The author, Helen Nardecchia, at 18

Dedicated to

the family

Author's Note

My mother's stories told to me in my youth with earnest excitement and fervor have come back to me in this collection of events and happenings. I am privileged to be the author of this collection. I want to thank family members and friends who contributed to its creation, and will forever appreciate their support.

Acknowledgement

This book is a documentary of lives, starting with grandparents who came from Germany and Italy. They established homes and families in America under difficult conditions with unquestionable love and determination. The names of family members are authentic and based on true-life events that bring the mystery of New Orleans and the whirlwind of Chicago alive.

Remembering
Those Who Came Before

Juliana Eiler,
mother of Augustine

Philip Eiler, father of Augustine

Augustine Eiler Zimardo,
daughter of Juliana

Joseph Dunn, Sr.
Augustine's first husband

Joseph and Augustine

Jasper Zimardo,
Augustine's second husband
the author's father

The author's brothers with Carl Dunn,
brother of Joseph Dunn, Sr.

Chapter 1

"Come on, Helen, get your boots on. We'll be late for school," Marie yells from the porch of the rented flat. In 1936, we lived in the back half of a seven-room apartment that was divided into two smaller apartments. We managed, but it felt very small with six of us crowded into three rooms.

"I'm coming, I'm coming," I yell back from the bedroom while tugging at leggings and a heavy winter jacket. My scarf, half twisted around my coat collar, hangs to the floor as I bend over to buckle my galoshes.

"Now stay with them, Frank," Mom's voice booms from the kitchen. "And if I hear that you ran off and left them alone one more time, I'll brain you."

No one trifled with Mom. Sometimes she chased Frankie around the dining room table because of his devilment, but in the end he always made her laugh by acting goofy or saying something hilariously funny. He knew her weaknesses. Sometimes he made her laugh until tears ran down her face and she had to cross her legs to keep from soaking her bloomers.

I rush outside to catch up with my sister Marie. The smell of smoke from potbellied stoves fills our lungs and an already polluted Chicago sky as families all over the city prepare for another cold November day. Sparkling icicles cover the trees. A foot of snow that fell during the night blankets the sidewalks, and cars creep along the slippery streets as children trudge to school.

I see Frank half a block ahead, waiting impatiently. He's already been up for hours delivering morning newspapers before going to school. Mom always helps him wrap half the batch the night before, then bundles him up before facing the bitter cold. Six o'clock every morning, he pulls his red wagon out from under the back stairs, loads the newspapers on, and then treks through the nearby neighborhoods in the thick snow placing one after another on front porches. He works proudly, never complaining, and he always turns over his earnings of five or six dollars a week to Mom.

Frank stomps his feet to keep warm and I catch up, admiring my big brother. He's such a handsome boy, almost pretty. We smile at each other and the three of us race to school, looking forward to getting in out of the cold.

With their curly brown hair and blue eyes, Frank and Marie always caught the eye of people passing by, who commented on what beautiful children Mom had. Mom generally answered, "I have four beautiful children." This always made me feel better.

After a while, Marie didn't always enjoy the compliments and sometimes stuck her tongue out at them if the mood struck her. Mom never stopped complaining about that.

Mom always had an eye out for an opportunity, and kept our health and well-being in mind. One day, she spotted an old two-wheeler within her price range at the Goodwill where she often shopped. She persuaded the owner to take a dollar for it and brought it home for Frank. He rode his bike confidently now every morning, except for the time the temperature dropped to five below zero and he returned home frozen to his bike.

Frank and Joe in New Orleans in 1923

Joe Dunn, 1927

"Mom!" He yelled many times until she finally heard him. Looking over banister, she spotted the problem. Frank's pants were frozen to the bike seat. Grabbing her coat and a blanket, she slowly started down the slippery stairs, clinging to the ice-coated railing. Mom was a big woman, a good five feet eight inches tall with an all-up-front stomach and long, thin legs. A fall could cripple her for life. So she took extra care inching down the icy stairs.

"Gotta get someone to spread gravel over these stairs," she grumbled. Stepping off the final stair, she tiptoed over the ice-spiked grass and threw the warm blanket around her son.

Mom always carried the basement key in her coat pocket to keep it handy for hanging sheets and bedding on the long lines strung in the basement, especially in the wintertime. Opening the door, she dragged Frank into the basement where the icicles around his hat and gloves could thaw.

"You're going to be okay, Frank, don't worry," she said as she wrapped the blanket tighter around him. But his red, frozen face worried her. That afternoon, she trotted over to the Goodwill to find long underwear, a scarf, and warmer clothing for Frank to wear while delivering papers. She felt very relieved when the red spots on his face disappeared and he could wiggle his fingers and toes again. Early the next morning found him back on the job, only snuggled up a bit warmer in long underwear.

Daddy, now, was another matter. We could hear him coughing many mornings. His bronchitis acted up at different times of the year, and he seemed to cough and spit more when the weather turned damp and wet. Mom always stoked the coals in the stove to warm the house more, but actually on a very cold morning only the kitchen ever felt the heat. The rest of the house just remained frigid until the extreme temperatures outside subsided. But the whole house always got warm and toasty when she put the oven on to bake.

One cold morning, Daddy decided to go about finding a job again. He had a few leads in the past, but they didn't work out. I could hear him telling Mom in the kitchen about approaching the Works Progress Administration program. The Roosevelt administration designed this program, commonly known as the WPA, to help people get back into the work force during the Depression. Dad had worked several different jobs but his lack of education and bad health prevented him from steady work.

"Augustine," he said to our mother, "I'm going to give this a try. But it's mostly outdoor work and I don't know how long I'll last."

Shaking her head up and down as she struck a match to light the oven, Mom also wondered how long it would last. "Give it a try, Jasper," she said as she continued to roll and flatten the bread dough on our tabletop. "I'll get you some long underwear tomorrow, too, and we'll do our best to bundle you up. Why don't you come with me to the Goodwill for a heavy pair of shoes?" I don't think we could have existed without the Goodwill.

Daddy knew he had to feed his family and do whatever it took to make ends meet. Thinking maybe the WPA could be the answer, he shaved and dressed carefully that morning, when snow covered the streets and frost wrapped the bathroom window, backing it until the spring thaw. No car in the family meant getting out early to traipse on the crunchy snow along with other Chicagoans who took crowded streetcars and waited in long lines, hoping to get hired. When we got home from school that evening, we heard good news. Daddy got a job.

As Mom cleans up after dinner, Marie and I drag our school books onto the kitchen table and begin our homework. Marie, or Mae, as we sometimes call her, is in fourth grade and I'm in second at Precious Blood School. Mom likes to call her Mae, but she's always Marie to me. Come to think of it, Joe, our oldest brother, called her Mae also.

Anyway, I'm a fairly good student, but Marie is advanced. We both made our First Holy Communion last May, and they chose Marie to crown the Blessed Mother. In the majestically quiet church, we watched proudly as she placed the wreath of tiny roses mixed with baby's breath on Mary's head after gently genuflecting in front of the Blessed Sacrament. Dressed in a white dress and veil, her natural curly brown hair hung softly on her shoulders and framed the rosy cherub face.

I watched in awe, wishing I had been selected.

14

"Mom, will you ask me these questions?" I quickly ask. Mom takes the book in her hand and begins drilling me as Marie writes math answers on her paper. Occasionally, Mom turns to stoke the potbellied stove to keep the kitchen warm, but I can tell something's on her mind. Later, Marie whispers to me that Mom is worried about our brother, Joe, who's seventeen and looking for a job.

Joe is a little over six feet tall now and not the lanky kid with the long wool stockings and cap any more. He's straight and lean with brown hair and wears his clothes well. The wonderful, generous thing about Joe is his broad smile. Somehow, his bright white teeth make his eyes sparkle each time he laughs. And he laughs a lot. He has a comical friend, Victor, who loves to entertain him, and together they are hell bent on telling one story after another to keep their lives carefree, in spite of the poverty and depression of the 1930s. Joe comes and goes very quietly and at times, we hardly know he's around.

A friend has told him about a leather company that's hiring, but it's night work, and Mom feels that a young man shouldn't have to sleep all day and work all night. However, times are hard and we need the money badly: Joe's salary would be a tremendous help.

Finally, it's bedtime and Mom says, "Okay, girls, enough studying for tonight. I will help you again in the morning, Helen."

"Can we have a snack?" asks Marie. Removing the wax paper from the plate of apple squares she made that morning, Mom says "Here" and gives each of us a piece with a glass of milk. What a delight to peel the slices of apples covered with cinnamon off the top and slowly slip them into my mouth.

As we crawl into bed and wrap the quilts around us, we hear footsteps on the stairs and a pounding on the porch. Both Joe and Frank are listening to Jack Armstrong on the radio in the back bedroom, so we know someone else is knocking the snow off their shoes, someone willing to walk up a flight of slippery stairs on a sub-zero evening. When we hear a knock on the curtained glass door that Mom always closes after dinner, we peek out over our covers to see who it is.

Mom pulls back the curtain and sees a smiling Bill Martin and another man standing there, both expelling great amounts of cold air. She unlocks and opens the door. Bill's been the Democratic Precinct Captain for several years now and the election is not far off.

"Hi, Mrs. Zimardo. We haven't had this much snow in November for a long time. Just thought I'd talk to you about voting in a couple of days. Is Jasper home?" asks Bill.

"Yes he is," answers Mom. "Come in."

Hearing the voices in the kitchen, our father comes in from the living room holding the newspaper. He shakes hands with both men and offers them each a kitchen chair. Bill Martin opened his overcoat and sat, but his friend preferred to stand. Mom stayed back by the stove to listen.

"Our Presidential election is next Tuesday, Jasper, and besides Roosevelt, we have several good men we'd like to see in office," says Bill Martin. "Oh, by the way this is Jerry McLean and he's running for State Representative, and if there's anything, anything at all that you need, Jasper, you can call on him or me. So it's important that you get out and vote. Here's a little something for your time and effort."

Bill Martin winks, shakes his head up and down in a quick sporadic way, and hands Dad an envelope. It's usually a five-dollar bill. At first, Dad doesn't say anything, but as Bill starts to take his leave, he comments dubiously. "I just got a job with the WPA, but with my health, I don't know if I can work outdoors."

"The WPA is mostly outdoor work, Jasper, but I'll see what I can do for you. I'll get back to you in a couple of days." With that the three men shake hands again. Bill Martin and the hopeful State Representative leave.

After they're gone, Daddy's usual swearing and raving begins.

"That bastard's not going to do a damn thing for me. He can take this five-dollar bill and shove it! As for that Roosevelt, I'm not voting for that bastard either." Mom just shakes her head, accustomed to Daddy's outbursts. She knows the five dollars will go into his pocket and he will show up at the polling place as usual, but will never tell who got his vote.

The kitchen quiets down and we drift off to sleep, lulled by the faint murmurs of our parents' continuing conversation. Another day ends on Claremont Street.

Chapter 2

Jasper and Augustine Zimardo, our parents, came from New Orleans to Chicago in the early 1920s with two boys, Joe and Frank. Born in Sicily, Dad came to the United States with his parents, Frank and Mary Zimardo, when he was six years old. Frank and Mary had three more sons in Amite, Louisiana, and two daughters in New Orleans. Back home in Sicily the family owned a strawberry farm, which may have inspired them to open a grocery store when they arrived in New Orleans.

Once settled in New Orleans, our grandparents started a store in produce and then gradually added additional savory items like canned plum tomatoes, tomato paste, olive oils, vinegars, and other Italian favorites that customers requested. The store thrived nicely with my Dad's parents at the helm. The boys, Mike, Joe, Tony, and Daddy, took over as they grew up. The girls, Mary and Therese, married and raised families. Mary eventually moved to California. Unfortunately, my grandmother Mary passed away when in her early fifties. The boys did their best to carry on the tradition of her friendly, gregarious treatment of customers.

Mom loved to talk about her past years in New Orleans. Grandpa Zimardo was a favorite subject of hers because of his colorful character. She remembered the day she made pasta sauce for the first time. Not really knowing where to start or end, she created the whole sauce with ketchup. When he tasted it, he cringed.

"No, no! Stupido," he said in his Italian accent. The next day, he dragged her into the kitchen.

"I teach you how to make sauce. First, go the olive oil in the bottom of the pan. Then, the onion and the garlic..." As he explained each step, he showed her what to do.

After her first lesson, Mom never used ketchup again, and Italian spaghetti reigned in our house once a week. Daddy made especially good sauce, and if he didn't get compliments after he got through preparing dinner, he didn't cook again for a long while.

Another time, Grandpa, now close to eighty years old, cleaned up from head to toe, shined his shoes, and dressed up in his best clothes to leave for a weekend. When my parents were first married, Mom questioned Dad about his absences.

"Where does he go every Friday and stay a whole weekend?"

Dad wouldn't say specifically, or only muttered "I don't know" as he angrily banged a pot or anything he had in his hands down on a counter. Clearly, Dad and his brothers were pretty disgusted with Grandpa. Mom wondered until Thelma, her neighbor, said one Monday, "We saw Mr. Zimardo in the French Quarter yesterday with a young woman on his arm." Suddenly Mom understood where Grandpa went on his weekends.

While Mom was pregnant with Frankie, Grandpa Zimardo passed away. Mike, Joe, and Jasper decided to close the store and each brother went his separate way. Mike, a twin of Joe, had acute asthma and moved to Tucson, Arizona, at his doctor's suggestion, and Joe relocated to California. Theresa remained in New Orleans, but Mary followed Joe to California.

After Daddy married, he decided to take his family to warmer climates because of the constant coughing spells the dampness of Louisiana encouraged. Actually, he had an affliction from a bullet wound he received helping a friend elope many years before. While Daddy held the ladder, the father of the girl fired his rifle and hit Dad in the chest, leaving him scarred for life and living with a debilitating bronchial condition. As a result, doctors sometimes misdiagnosed him with tuberculosis.

Mom never held back stories of her early childhood or her later years. As we grew up, she repeated the same stories often, but we never got tired of hearing them. Most interesting were her years before she met Daddy.

She was born August 6, 1896, to Philip and Juliana Eiler in New Orleans, Louisiana, and named Augustine Mary. She came last in a family of seven children: Julia, the oldest, followed by Katie, Amelia, Laura, Caroline, Philip, and finally, Augustine. In her growing-up years, many friends called her Gussie.

Our maternal grandparents both came from Bavaria, Germany, and met on the boat coming to America. The boat docked in New Orleans; Grandpa Eiler liked New Orleans and stayed. He later learned that Grandma Eiler's family remained in New Orleans as well. Determined to find her, he searched all possible records with the result that they finally met and married.

Grandpa Eiler, a shoemaker, set up a shop next to their home on Rampart Street, supporting the family comfortably with his trade. Grandma Eiler was a homemaker who reared her family as peacefully and comfortably as possible. Many New Orleans families in the early 1900s had black nannies, and Mom made a point to tell us in her stories that they always had a nanny in their home to help with household chores and raise children.

Five girls later, Grandma and Grandpa Eiler celebrated the birth of a son. They named him Philip, after his father, but he suffered poor health from birth on and he died at the young age of twenty-one, leaving the grieving family of girls growing up in the German lifestyle guided by the strength of both their parents.

Grandma Eiler, or Juliana, as she preferred to be called, now in the twilight years of her marriage and thinking her fertile days were behind her, was completely surprised when the doctor told her she was pregnant again. She ignored her morning discomfort and afternoon sleepiness, blaming it on this and that. Nine months passed, and another little girl entered the Eiler family. They named her Augustine Mary because she was born in the month of August. Afterward, my mother loved to tell people, with an outburst of laughter, that she was a "change-of-life baby." She liked the idea that it made her sound different.

Juliana's older girls were already married by the time Augustine was born, building families of their own, and so my mother grew up in a loving home with cousins for playmates and lots of attention from all.

Mom never failed to tell her favorite Mardi Gras stories, and how the exhilaration of all the children mounted as the days drew near. She was just a youngster, maybe nine or ten, when taken to the French Quarter to see the costumes and the crowds of people that turned out for the celebration. The masks especially worried her because some of them were terribly scary.

As she followed the crowd, Augustine strayed a bit from her companions and found herself in the middle of an unruly pack who wore skeleton masks, dangling beads, and artificial animal heads. She trembled and her heart pounded while looking around for someone she might recognize. As she turned, a large bare-chested black man wearing a half mask and deep red lipstick flashed his face in hers and yelled "Boo!"

She screamed and luckily ran into her cousin, who had been looking for her. Each time she told the tale she'd say the same thing, "I'll never forget it. It was the scariest thing that ever happened to me." And Grandma Eiler refused to let her go again. If she ever returned to Mardi Gras, and it's quite possible she did in later years, it would have been as an adult or after Grandma Eiler had passed on.

We also loved to hear about the Negro funerals in New Orleans. The old and the young lined the streets watching as they carried their loved ones to the cemetery. It was a very solemn occasion, Mom said. The pallbearers slowly trekked down the street with the heavy coffin on their shoulders following the band that played forlorn, desperate music, exemplifying the sadness of the day while the black people hummed mournfully.

After the burial, the entire theme changed. The band played Dixieland music and the people strummed and danced back down the same road to celebrate with food and drinks. It ended as a jubilant occasion and the crowds lining the streets loved it.

In the meantime, Grandpa Eiler, or at times we may call him Philip, continued to repair shoes until one day a stranger walked into his shop and asked him to consider making false limbs. He felt overjoyed once he started creating these artificial parts, but he got so busy he never had time to repair his family's shoes, so down to the corner shoemaker they'd all trot. Fascinated with the learning process, he spent days and nights perfecting his techniques. His business grew from word of mouth and people came to him from all over. One man had several appointments over the months while Grandpa meticulously fitted him with a false leg that connected to the thigh. Mom said that until the day he died, he prided himself on that accomplishment.

Grandpa Eiler often came running into the kitchen, face beaming with excitement, carrying an artificial leg and foot that looked positively human. He even added the realistic rose of flesh color to the knee, Mom said.

"Julie," he'd yell. "Look, look how perfect this looks. What do you think?"

Generally, Grandma Eiler felt so amazed by what she saw that she hardly responded. Truly, he had found his calling.

Sadly, though, Philip's heart gave out over time and he died at the relatively young age of fifty-nine. Augustine was in her late teens. However, she and her mother remained in their home on Rampart Street in New Orleans with the rest of the family living nearby except Aunt Katie, who eventually moved to Biloxi, Mississippi. Apparently the only sister unable to have children, Aunt Katie adopted a little girl and named her Ruth. I can remember Aunt Katie and Ruth visiting us many years later in Chicago on Claremont Street. I could swear Ruth had an Asian background, for her features looked very oriental, but I never heard the subject brought up or out to confirm that.

Ruth and Aunt Katie

At nineteen or twenty Mom met Joe Dunn—through friends, I imagine. We have no record of how she met him. She worked for a Jewish firm where, we assume, she got her background in sales, because later on she became a successful saleswoman for Maison Blanche, one of New Orleans' top department stores. Joe might have worked as a salesman in one form or another until he got a factory job some time later.

Joseph Thomas Dunn was born a devout Irish Catholic who attended Mass every morning. The Eiler family was Lutheran. Mom, dressed in long skirts and starched blouses, attended services in the Lutheran Church regularly with Grandma Eiler, lifting their voices to high pitch with "Just a Closer Walk With

23

Thee," "Amazing Grace," and "The Old Rugged Cross." Grandma Eiler, a heavy-set German lady, always looked neat and orderly in her billowy dresses, which covered her to the ankles as she held on firmly to the pew in front of her. Occasionally, she'd lean slightly toward her daughter's tall, slender form. In those days Augustine always wore a wide-brimmed hat that encircled her long red curly hair.

All through our growing-up years, Mom liked to sit at the piano, when the mood struck her, and play those favorite old hymns she used to sing in New Orleans with her mother. Then she'd close up the piano and not go near it for a long time.

Graduation day for Helen's brother Frankie
at age 15 or 16, June 1938.

First Communion for Marie and Helen, June 1938
Photo taken same day as Frankie's graduation
photo on facing page.

Chapter 3

We never really knew when Mom began to wear glasses, but assume it happened after she entered the working world. We have a few photos of her without them before she married, but I remember her always wearing glasses and wide-brimmed hats.

As she and Joe dated, Mom became interested in his religion. Maybe his steady example of daily Mass and Holy Communion impressed her, or perhaps she felt disenchanted with her own church. At any rate, she began to accompany him to Sunday Mass, and sometimes, unbeknownst to him, visited the church during the week. She told us the story about the homeless man more than once and I'm quite sure I'll never forget it.

"It was a blistery cold day in New Orleans with a chill-driven rain that cut through outer garments and wormed its way through skin and bones," she said. "I walked up the brick stairs of the church and saw a man shivering in the corner of the doorway. He was poorly dressed with long, gray, dirty hair and badly in need of a bath. Even his shoes were worn to the point that his feet stuck out. I had seen him before but he never stood close enough to speak to, but this time we made eye contact.

"Where's your coat?" I asked.

"Don't have one." He answered as he shivered.

"Come inside the church where it's warmer," I insisted by holding the door open for him to enter.

"I can't. I was told not to go inside the church. People don't like seeing me hang around in there." He said with chattering teeth.

"Well!" said I, "you wait here and I will be right back."

Two blocks down from the church was a clothing store. I found my way to the store and back to the church with a bundle under my arm.

"Here," I said, handing the bundle to him. Inside were a pair of long underwear and warm socks that I had bought. "Now, you go into the men's washroom and put those on right now," I commanded, holding the church door open for him. Tears ran down his face as he thanked me. When I left the church, he was gone."

My sister and I really felt Mom loved telling this story. It demonstrated her strength and courage that shone through that day.

She noticed not only the peace and contentment of her daily visits to the church, but also the passion she felt when kneeling before the altar and tabernacle. Her body felt excitement as well as sorrow each time she elevated her eyes to the striking image of the Crucifix hanging above the altar, and the sparkling gold of the Tabernacle. Never before had she experienced such a dedication; never before a desire to return daily to such a peaceful environment. She attended day in and day out until she was captured.

Upon exploring, she discovered that convert classes were held once a week in the evening and she joined. The classes lasted eight weeks and she attended faithfully, asking Aunt Julia to sit with Grandma Eiler while she was gone.

"Where you going?" asked Aunt Julia sarcastically.

Patiently, Mom always said, "To convert classes. I'm becoming a Catholic." Smug and sassy, Julia replied, "Isn't your religion good enough for you?"

And Mom heard this same tirade each week before leaving for classes.

From what we can gather, none of the other sisters were as critical as Aunt Julia. Julia's one daughter, Thelma, was close to our mother's age and never left her mother's side. What one didn't think of, the other did. So together, they harassed Mom about leaving the Lutheran religion and becoming a Catholic.

All through Lent, Mom put up with this aggravation until her final acceptance into the Catholic Church in 1916. She kept it a secret from Joe until Easter Sunday morning.

"I'll go to church with you tomorrow, Joe," Augustine said.

Easter Sunday dawned bright and glorious as the women showed off their lovely frocks and large hats. Pompadours and long curls were the fashion, as well as bright colors and polka dots. People who hadn't gone to church all year dressed lavishly, with some men in white suits, spats, and straw hats. According to Mom, it was something to see, and Joe looked very handsome.

And so he was: tall with dark hair, fine features, and a warm smile, judging from the one picture she had of him. She kept it for years in her jewelry box. They were very much in love and when Communion time came during the Mass and Augustine followed him up to the railing to receive the body of Christ, he felt overwhelmed with joy when she said, "It's all right, Joe. I'm a Catholic now."

Later that same year—as a matter of fact—it was December 1, 1916—he presented her with a Manual of Prayers and signed it:

> *God be with you*
> *from Joseph T. Dunn*
> *to Augustine Eiler*

As I cradle it in my hands now and look at its aged condition, barely holding together, tears fill my eyes to think how precious it must have been to her when he presented it. She pasted two prayers in it and the following, called "Affliction," must have been her favorite because of its power.

God would not send you the darkness, dear
If He felt you could bear the light
But you would not cling to His guiding hand,
If the way was always bright.
And you would not care to walk by faith
Could you always walk by sight.
Tis true, He has many an anguish for your sorrowful heart to bear

28

Many a cruel thorn crown for your tired head to wear.
But He knows how few would reach Heaven at all,
If pain did not guide them there.
So he sends you the blinding darkness and the furnace of
seven-fold heat.
Tis the only way, believe me, to keep you close to His feet.
For 'tis always so easy to wander, when our lives are glad and
sweet.
Then, nestle your hand in your Father's and sing if you can as
you go.
Your song may cheer some one behind you whose courage is
sinking low.
And what if your lips do quiver, God will love you better so.

Augustine and Joe were married June 21, 1918.

She was three months pregnant by the following September,
and four months later he was dead.

Joe had a heart murmur. It didn't seem serious to them at the
time. Lots of folks live long lives with a heart murmur. But Joe's
working conditions didn't help his health. His factory job subjected
him to standing in water and it took its toll after a number of years.
Pneumonia took his life.

In addition, Mom repeatedly told us the story about the floods
that came to New Orleans that year, causing an influenza epidemic
that killed hundreds of people. Joe needed a doctor badly as he ran
a high fever and coughed night after night during the heavy rains.
Leaving him in Grandma Eiler's care, Mom donned heavy boots,
an old coat, and a hat and waded through the flooded streets until
she arrived at Dr. Gladstone's house, a good three blocks away.
She recalls:

"Dr. Gladstone had a rowboat in an old shed behind his house.
"Let's take it, Augustine," he said. I was so glad not to have to
walk that long flooded way home. We saw many homes with water
up to the windows of their living rooms. People were desperate and
crying. By the time we got to Rampart Street, the water was waist
high.

But for Joe, it was too late. The doctor couldn't save him. He died that night in Augustine's arms. With only seven months of living and loving, this part of her life ended. She grieved and Grandma Eiler grieved. Grandma was too old to survive the tragedy. She couldn't have asked for a better son-in-law. She loved him and her grief finally took her. Augustine and Joseph Dunn's son was born April 8, 1919, and Grandma Eiler passed away the end of that same year. Mom's story was two-fold as she told us the details.

"The birth was hard. Even the doctor wondered if I'd make it. "It's a big baby," he told me. And so I labored for hours. Grandma Eiler, sickly and tearful, prayed and paced from the kitchen to the living room while the doctor shook his head hoping for a safe birth. The sweat poured from his forehead as he used some sort of instruments to bring Joe down into the birth canal. Julia had run for Dr. Gladstone and I could see her standing at the foot of the bed terrified.

Finally, after suffering pain beyond endurance, this child's great big head emerged, tearing tissue and strength from my body. I was told later my screams were heard at every house on Rampart Street. It was a boy. Sucking his fingers and yelling for food, he was placed in my arms—looking exactly like his father. Only a few months later, holding Joseph Thomas Dunn, Jr. our son in my arms, I again wore black and watched as Grandma Eiler was laid to rest.

Chapter 4

Her new-found faith or the Affliction prayer must have sustained Augustine during the turmoil and sorrow of 1918, because she never faltered—she just pressed on. On April 27, Baby Joseph was baptized at St. Thomas Church in New Orleans. She moved in with Aunt Julia and took care of her little boy until he was a year old. Then, with money running low, she approached Aunt Julia one day about taking care of Joe while she went to work. Aunt Julia, not always approachable, agreed to the plan, but expressed little enthusiasm about the idea.

"I don't know, Augustine," she said. "He's a handful."

Reluctantly, Julia gave it a try and, with a friend's encouragement, Augustine applied for a salesperson's job at Maison Blanche. They hired her. But her daily routine was not easy and Aunt Julia complained constantly at the end of the day. Poor little Joe was either "a big cry baby" or "dirtied his pants just too often to suit me." Augustine felt desperate but stuck it out because she had no alternative.

After two years of putting up with Aunt Julia's degrading remarks of "You're in this situation because you gave up your true religion. God is punishing you," or "Stay home and take care of your own damn kid," she felt even more hopeless and depressed than she did right after her husband died. Clearly, something needed to change, so she accepted a date arranged by a fellow salesperson and friend who frequented the Zimardo grocery store and knew Jasper Zimardo.

31

"Jasper's really a nice guy, Gussie. He's a hard worker. His family owns a grocery store. You'll like him."

As it turned out, Jasper really was a nice guy. Thirty-five and single, he was nice-looking too, with brown curly hair just beginning to recede, and always warm and friendly. Augustine enjoyed his company, especially when they visited his big Italian family. And she appreciated how nice he was to Joe. He often said, "Forget Julia, let's take him with us." After they'd dated a while, Joe accompanied them wherever they went. Jasper began to treat him like his own son and Augustine liked that.

Finally, when Joe was three years old, Jasper said, very casually, "Let's get married," and she said, "Yes."

Dressed in a blue summer suit and white wide-brimmed hat surrounded with feathers and flowers, Mom said, "I do" to a suave Jasper Zimardo groomed in a gray serge suit and a pink boutonniere.

It was a good marriage. Daddy sometimes got frustrated and annoyed with Joe, but no more than he would have with a child of his own or any three-year-old. Daddy could get excitable, but when the dust settled, his warm nature came through and the problem ended. He never nagged or threatened. Suddenly at thirty-five, his life changed from that of carefree bachelor to a responsible husband and father. The grocery store supported them comfortably, but it all ended when Grandpa Zimardo died. With Daddy's health in jeopardy, the family sold the store. Actually, Uncle Mike and Uncle Joe wanted to move on anyway, and Daddy's two sisters, Mary and Therese, didn't want the store either.

But now Jasper had to find another means of supporting his family. He had the grocery truck, which encouraged him to apply for a candy salesman job. Every day, he packed up the truck with boxes of candy and drove to all the stores and cafes on his list. He did well at this endeavor, but again his poor health began to interfere. His constant coughing made it obvious that he needed a drier climate, and the doctors reinforced that conclusion.

It was now 1923, the warm month of June. Azaleas bloomed all over New Orleans in all their breathtaking beauty. Early-morning workers scurried across Canal Street catching streetcars while Mom once again screamed with contractions in a little house on a corner as Daddy paced the floors. This time the delivery went much easier for her. Frankie weighed less than Joe and seemed more anxious to come into a big world. He arrived in a matter of a few hours and Daddy's eyes filled with tears and excitement as he saw his first-born son.

Trying desperately to make a go of it in New Orleans went nowhere, with no one to turn to. Their first move to Biloxi, Mississippi, may have happened because of Aunt Katie's encouragement, or Daddy may have thought his candy business would do better there because of a few successful clients. We really aren't sure, but we do know that they didn't stay long. And Daddy continued to cough.

So after some deliberation, having heard that Texas had a drier climate, they packed up the truck again and moved to San Antonio, Texas. Mom recalled the day:

"I couldn't believe the heat the day we arrived. It was late July. I felt we had just stepped into an oven as we felt the tires of the truck sink into hot tar on the streets. I couldn't imagine anyone wanting to live here. New Orleans had its hot days, too, but not like this."

The overpowering heat played a dominant role in their leaving San Antonio, but Daddy probably also had problems finding clients. The candy business, evidently, didn't thrive very well due to the heat, which probably melted the chocolate bars on more than one occasion. The boys were little then. Joe may have been six or seven and Frankie two years old at the most.

Then they got in touch with Carl Dunn, Joe Dunn Senior's brother. Mom remembered that he lived in Chicago, so she wrote him. He lived on the north side of Chicago and, according to our mother, was a Communist. He encouraged them to come north. So again, they packed up the truck and they left the heat of San Antonio, with a dream of a better employment opportunity and more suitable weather for Daddy's health. The struggle continued in many aspects of their life after arriving, but they knew one thing for certain. They had to make the most of it because moving again, in Mom's eyes, was out of the question. "We had moved enough,"

Mom said pensively. She was much happier living in a place with the four seasons of spring, summer, fall, and winter. And she finally came to the conclusion that it didn't matter where Daddy lived, he'd always cough.

Now a new life in the Midwest began. Carl Dunn, connected to a group of activists, came in contact with many people. Through these contacts, Mom began to take in boarders. Carl even worked on Daddy, trying to convince him to join the Communist Party, but our parents never seriously considered this. They may have struggled, but they loved America too much to ever turn their back on its beliefs. Mom respected the boarders as human beings and appreciated the extra money they brought into the house. Daddy took any job he could get to help bring in money to support his wife and boys, but he never seemed to make enough. Sometimes he even worked two jobs, but his poor health often intervened.

Finally, after Carl's steady badgering and harassment, Mom began to worry that Daddy might weaken. She considered it wise to move. Carl seemed determined to get our Dad into the Communist fold. Somehow, they learned about an apartment on the west side of Chicago and investigated. Mom asked her boarders to find another place to live and they departed the north side, leaving Carl Dunn to his own devices.

Once again, Mom, Dad, and the boys packed up and moved. This time it was to a flat on Harrison Street, probably not far from Western Avenue, and they enrolled Joe in Precious Blood School. Every morning he donned his knickers, wool socks, jacket, and cap to attend classes. The nuns liked him because he was bright. He was also "headstrong," as Mom said, but she understood him and went out of her way to suit him. "He's not only a good-looking boy but a good boy," she told her friends. Each day he reminded her more of his father. Whenever Daddy vented his anger about something Joe did, she defended her son, who liked to spend countless hours pacing the floor and thinking.

The word "suit" reminds me of a story she loved to tell. For more than one special occasion at school, Mom visited the Goodwill for men's suits and remade them to fit Joe. She excelled at this. After a while, she started doing the same thing for Frankie.

Some of the suits were expensively tailored in the finest of material. One of the nuns asked him one day where he got the suit he was wearing and he said, "My mother made it." That evening, he told Mom how much Sister Josephine liked his suit. She smiled with a sense of pride, especially since she knew it had cost not much more than a dollar.

Daddy fared pretty well in Chicago. He had bouts of coughing spells during the damp, rainy season, but the cold seemed to help him. He had a factory job and found himself able to work steadier hours.

Just as the spring of the year began to surface with signs of green grass sprouting and trees starting to bud, Mom's nine months of pregnancy ended and Marie Therese was born March 28, 1928. After the two boys, both Mom and Dad felt delighted to have a little girl and a very pretty one, at that. Her curly hair and pudgy red cheeks turned heads as Mom wheeled the buggy and shopped the nearby stores with Joe, now nine years old, and Frankie, five.

But then once again, she heard "You're pregnant, Mrs. Zimardo," when Mom told the doctor she felt tired and nauseated. It was not a good time to be pregnant. In 1930, right after the stock market crash, the nation had closed down and massive layoffs occurred. Marie was two years old and their living conditions needed improvement because of tight quarters. Daddy joined the ranks of the layoffs and stood in line looking for employment as the Great Depression spread across our country.

But life goes on and December 14th brought forth another little girl—a very tiny one this time.

"We were so sure it would be a boy," Mom told her neighbor. "We only thought about boy's names and decided on Philip. When the nurse brought her to me and said we need a name for her birth certificate, I had none. I said "What's your name?" and she said Helene. I thought that was pretty and so we named her Helene Ann."

December was a very cold month with Chicago's usual snow, ice, and wind and Daddy worried about keeping me warm. Wrapping me in mounds of blankets, he'd rock me in front of the stove in the kitchen, with only a tiny little face peeking out. Mom had to keep an eye on him because he often dropped off to sleep with me in his arms, and she feared I'd wind up on the floor. I was just weeks old.

I might have been three or four years old when we moved from Harrison Street into Lacocca's building on Claremont Street. The flat wasn't much bigger than before. The boys had to sleep on an old studio couch that Mom bought from Goodwill, but the rent was more affordable. Daddy continued to do odd jobs wherever he could find them, because the state of the country wasn't much better. Franklin Delano Roosevelt, as President, did his best to improve the economy and strived diligently to get Americans back to work. Eleanor Roosevelt toured the country countless times to witness the hunger and poverty of the American people. Reporting back to the President, she worked relentlessly to promote education, civil rights, and lifting people out of poverty.

It took time, but finally the economy began to turn around, and programs like the WPA helped put food on tables all over America. In November 1936 the presidential election occupied the minds of many citizens, including my parents.

Chapter 5

"Let's go, Jasper," Mom said. "We'll go shopping, get you a pair of heavy shoes, and then go to the polling place to vote." Daddy donned his heavy coat and cap. As they walked down the side passageway and half a mile to the Goodwill in the cold air, Mom decided to tell him about the landlady who owned the apartments next to theirs.

"Mrs. Pope is willing to convert her two apartments into one big apartment for us if we want it," said Mom.

Daddy listened and then asked, "How can she do that?"

"Just by opening the door that separates them and making a few adjustments."

"Yeah," said Daddy, "but how much rent does she want?"

"Maybe more than what we're paying now, but not too much more. And just think, Jasper, the boys will have a bedroom of their own and don't have to sleep on that uncomfortable couch any more." Daddy sounded convinced, and once again Mom began to think about boarders to help defray living costs. By opening up the two apartments, she gained an extra bedroom.

Since that subject succeeded, she decided to approach another.

"Joe is going with his friend, Victor, to see about that leather company job today. But it's not good for a young man to work nights."

Mom tucked close to Daddy, holding his arm so not to slip or slide on the ice. Finally Daddy said, "It won't hurt him. He better take what he can get."

Mom accepted that and after a good brisk walk, they entered the Goodwill.

After the move into the Popes' seven-room flat, Mom noticed that a young homeless man always slept in the building basement across the passageway from us. The passageway separated two large apartment buildings and was wide enough to hold a parked car. In fact, the older kids on the block played baseball there, hitting the ball like a bullet straight through to the street. "That's a home run, Freddie," shouted one of the boys. More than once, basement windows got broken because the ball didn't go straight through to the street, but zigzagged. This, understandably, annoyed the neighbors and the people living in the buildings.

The building on the right side of the passageway had a sunken basement, a cement foundation of about sixteen feet square, with a wrought-iron railing and cement stairs leading down to a storage room. Two Italian families lived in the large flats above. The homeless young man lived in the basement storage room, and no one knew where he came from. We only knew that his family had disowned him.

When Mom wanted to know something, she didn't hesitate— she got out there and found out all she could about "the poor fellow," as she called him. After talking to her landlord, Mrs. Pope, she discovered he was the age of her Joe, and that's all it took for her to help him out.

She decided to catch him by surprise after dinner one evening by actually knocking on the door of the storage room and asking, "What's your name, son?"

He answered, "Barkus."

Before we all realized it, Barkus moved into the spare bedroom. Mom even helped find him a job, which enabled him to pay board. I remember that he stayed with us a couple of years, until he had a confrontation with the man across the street. One summer night, with the sky showing off its blood-red full moon, we heard a tap on the back door. Mom pushed the curtain back and saw a sight. Opening the door quickly she said, "My God, what happened to you?"

Apparently, Barkus had been spreading rumors about the man's wife. Where he got his information, we'll never know, but the man and his brother watched for him this night and beat the tar out of him. His face was a mass of red blood. Mom soaked him down with baking soda and warm water, but his bruises hung around a very long time. Every glance in the mirror served as a reminder that he'd better keep his mouth shut from now on. And Mom warned him—oh, how she warned him!—about spreading rumors.

Barkus finally left our neighborhood after a while. He had designs on different girls on the block, but no one wanted him around, and we, as a family, finally complained to Mom about his living in the same house with us. Joe worked nights now and didn't notice much, but Marie and Frankie expressed strong concerns about Barkus and his carelessness. I was too young to absorb the damages of the situation. Mom's boarder had stayed long enough, in the eyes of her family, so she gave up on that idea for the present.

Besides, washing heavy blue jeans over a bathtub created enough of a strain when she only washed for two boys. Three was more than Mom could endure and often had Daddy help her. She didn't get a washing machine until years later.

Having four more rooms than before made the Christmas of 1936 much more festive. Bill Martin came through for Daddy this time and informed him of a job opening at a public school in the neighborhood that needed a night watchman. The family's financial situation, therefore, improved considerably. With Joe working steady now, two incomes made a big difference in the household.

A few days before Christmas, around nine o'clock in the

morning, Mom heard thump, thump, thump coming up two flights of stairs. Then Mom heard a whoosh on the porch. Wondering about Frankie's whereabouts after he finished delivering all his papers, she pulled open the back door to find him struggling with a five-foot-tall, long-needled Christmas tree. She saw her eager-beaver son standing with a wide grin on his face, One arm outstretched and the other straightening his wool hat as he tried to balance the tree. Curly hair all around and the brightest blue eyes brought tears to her eyes as he shouted, "Look, Mom. Mr. Ivino gave it to me."

Mr. Ivino owned the building next door and liked Frank. He set up a tent every year on an empty lot across from King School and filled it with Christmas trees. Getting close to Christmas, he decided to get rid of a few. Frank rode by the tent on his bike and stopped with longing in his heart, which probably showed in his eyes because he wasn't sure we could afford a tree. Mr. Ivino saw the longing and helped him tie the tree to his bike. Maybe it wasn't the most symmetrical tree around, and it certainly had its bare spots, but it looked perfect to us.

Mom loved to hug her family. When she tucked Frankie close and he saw her face brighten with a long, gentle smile, he knew he was loved. Off to the Goodwill she went again. This time she bought ornaments and decorations for the tree at five and ten cents each, even some a couple of pennies.

But the total joy, the absolute total joy, for me came from the miniature stove, refrigerator, table, and chairs, along with dishes or ironing board whatever she could afford, that Marie and I found Christmas morning surrounding the tree. Some items from rich homes and in perfect condition cost little or nothing where Mom shopped. "The rich kids just outgrew them," she always told us.

In summer we dragged the whole miniature kitchen out on the back porch, and every morning, as soon as Marie and I crawled out of bed, we played there for hours. I sometimes stayed up until midnight imagining stories and situations beyond belief, but Marie always gave up after a while and read instead. If rain wasn't in the forecast, we left the whole kitchen ensemble out on the porch and we'd begin again the next morning.

A couple of summers later, when we got a bit older and the nights got extremely warm, Mom even let us sleep out on the porch. I loved dragging an old mattress, blankets, and pillows out to watch the moon and stars fill the skies at night as I tucked all my dolls around me. Dad always checked to see that the gate across the stairs was locked, and he left the back door open so they could hear any disturbances.

Where have all the little girls gone, long time coming.

Where have they all gone, long time ago.

Chapter 6

She was slender and beautiful with coal-black hair and a waistline nineteen inches at the most. "He's in love," Frankie told Mom. We began to see our brother, Joe, smile more and even laugh out loud as he strolled around the house on his days off.

"Twenty years old and already in love. What's this all about?" Daddy asked.

Knowing how temperamental Daddy could get at times, Mom decided to keep the subject low-key to prevent ruffling his feathers.

"Oh, he just met her. Victor told Frankie she's a very nice girl. Don't get excited," answered Mom.

Joe and his friend Victor had worked the night shift for the leather company over a year now, almost two really. Some days, instead of sleeping in, the two went to the roller rink. Victor the clown made Joe laugh constantly, as well as the rest of us when we gathered around the kitchen table. Victor was Italian and lived across the alley from us. We had a tall fort fence surrounding our back yard and an alley on the other side of the fence that ran from Flournoy Street all the way down to Taylor, with several houses on both sides.

Mom worried, though. Even though she convinced Daddy that it was just a fleeting friendship, she knew Joe to be a very serious and sensitive young man. Joe couldn't simply have a "fleeting friendship" with a girl. He was either in or out of love—nothing in between for him. So Mom continued to pump Frank.

"This girl, Frank. How often does he see her?"

"Every time they go to the rink, Mom."

"Couple of times a week?"

"Yeah, I guess. Victor says her father is very strict, so she has to meet Joe at the rink. He can't go to her house."

Mom would store that for a while, then wait for another opportunity.

"Hey Frank, this girl Joe sees?"

"Yeah?"

"What's her name?"

"Mary something. She's got a long Italian name."

"Oh, she's Italian?"

"Yeah."

She never asked Joe any of these questions. A very private young man, he revealed nothing. And when Mom did attempt to question him, he simply wouldn't answer.

This went on for a long time. Mom picked up bits and pieces from Frank but obviously, Joe was smitten. We learned with time that he met her at a movie theater, met her at a park, also maybe someplace else other than the rink, because he was not allowed to pick her up at home. She had three sisters and a brother, all of whom had to sneak and lie to live peacefully in a stressful household. The daytime courtship continued with all of us knowing very little, except for what Joe told Frank.

         CB   CB   CB

While Mom pondered Joe's rendezvous, she neglected to notice a duel going on between our neighbor's grandson and me. A six- or seven-foot fort fence separated us from the adjoining home on our right, with a narrow passageway in between. I could have been no more that seven or eight years old when a continuous bickering with Paul reached a full crescendo. First we called each other names, then a small stone flew over, which admittedly, I initiated. Next, a large rock flew up and over just as I looked up and slammed across my nose.

I screamed and Paul ran. The summer warmth had most neighbors outdoors enjoying the eighty-degree temperatures, and while Mom visited on the front porch, someone ran to tell her about the small figure slumped against the back fence with blood squirting all over her and the ground. Mom rushed to my aid and to this day, I remember her carrying me up two flights of stairs as I held a blood-soaked towel to my face. Taking me to a hospital emergency room never crossed her mind—no one did that back then—and she applied warm compresses and home remedies until I settled down and fell asleep.

The next day, Paul's grandparents sent him up to apologize and we became the best of friends, despite the battle scar in the middle of my nose that still reminds me of our bitter conflict. Paul Amato never talked about his parents, but our neighborhood grapevine revealed that he and his two brothers, Vito and Freddie, lived in an orphanage until their grandparents took them. If I recall rightly, they stayed two years and we never learned what happened to them after they left. We heard rumored on the streets that they went up for adoption. Losing the boys must have hurt the grandparents, but surely separating the boys for different homes created more of a hardship.

ೞ   ೞ   ೞ

Chicago had short summers, but we all welcomed them with open arms even during the exceptionally hot days. Quick bolts of excitement buzzed along the street whenever one of the hefty fellows on the block, sweating profusely with wrench in hand, leisurely walked down to the corner fire hydrant.

Without a word, two or three others joined him, holding a

long, flat board. Everyone on the block knew what this meant, and the kids rushed home to put their bathing suits on. The men jammed the board into the mouth of the hydrant and the wrench loosened the dial after several attempts. Sometimes it took two or three fellows to turn the dial. But then, water cascaded over the board and everyone howled. Older folks watched as the young splashed and played under the spray that nearly reached the sky. Joy and laughter echoed down the street as young girls coming home from work in their nice frocks got dragged under the water by the frolicking young men. We always waited with bated breath as the handsomest fellow on the block dragged his best girlfriend under the water to hug and kiss her.

The taller kids liked to fling their legs over the board at the mouth of the hydrant, causing the water to lift them higher as they erupted with yells and laughter. I can remember Mom taking her shoes and socks off to walk along the curb where the water curled and ran down the street. She always held up her dress and squealed with delight as her toes twisted and splashed in the cool water. Daddy stood on the porch smiling and shaking his head at the whole sight.

But it always ended as fast as it got started. A police car inevitably pulled up and an officer, wrench in hand, got out to turn it off. Sadness reigned and faces drooped. Sometimes some brave soul shouted out, "Let it be. We're just having fun." We never knew if someone called the cops or if they just happened to ride by and catch us in the act. Regardless, we always remembered those happy moments as the highlight of our summer.

છ   છ   છ

Two or three years went by, and Joe continued to court Mary. He started to bring her over occasionally, giving us all a chance to get reasonably acquainted. He made a point to invite Victor also, so laughter and entertainment prevented any grave questions or conversation. Dad and Mom made it obvious that they didn't want Joe to consider marriage just yet. Daddy's night watchman job ended and again he had to find odd jobs to support the family. Clearly, they needed his income at home, but they also realized that Joe was serious about Mary.

Trying to suppress his anger, Daddy often dropped little remarks while sitting in his lounge chair. On some occasions, he started out quietly and then built up into strong outbursts.

"He makes a few bucks and right away he wants to get married."

Mom could be a million miles away mentally, but he'd keep at it until he brought her back.

"He knows we are strapped here, God damn it! A couple more years would help a lot."

"Who are you talking about?" Mom would ask, knowing all the while.

Then an explosion generally occurred that ended with Daddy sarcastically calling Joe "your son" and Mom saying to him that il figlio meant "your son" in Italian which, of course, referred to Frankie. Then the dust settled until the next time.

ᘓ ᘓ ᘓ

Frankie was beginning to grow up also. He had come a long way from the time when, one summer at a camp in Michigan, he impetuously ran up a ladder that fell down quickly at the other end to split his forehead open, scarring him for life. Mom weathered that storm, and the years in school when the nuns sent notes home to her at least once a week complaining about his behavior. To keep her sweet little boy from turning into a complete monster, all she had to do was tell the nun, "See that long ruler you have over there? Use it and stop sending me notes." He spent many a day in a corner of the classroom.

But an overnight tragic incident opened the door to maturity for Frank. He had been hopping freight cars with a couple of friends for some time. One day after school, he saw his buddy slip from the train and fall under its wheels. The scream that accompanied the fall filled Frank's ears and mind with horror. He rushed over and found the cut-up body. The terror that followed him as he ran home led him straight to the bathroom and he vomited. Mom held him tight as he relayed the story to her, trembling. Daddy fumed. After several sleepless nights, Frank's devilish tomfoolery subsided quickly and he began to apply himself at school. With graduation closing in on him, he decided that he wanted to attend St. Philip's High School.

Father Malacky offered to help Frank enroll at St. Philip's; he and Frank became friends when Frankie served as an altar boy. Grades were not the problem, since Frank was an A student. Our folks just couldn't afford to pay the tuition. Father Malacky explained to Mom that his grades could get him into the school on something comparable to the scholarships we know of today. And he did! However, he didn't bother to tell Frank or my parents that the scholarship only lasted a year.

Exactly one year later, our financial situation not having improved, Frank quit St. Philip's and enrolled in public school. During this time, he worked odd jobs. I remember one year he brought home a turkey for Thanksgiving. He made deliveries to a grocery store and the owner said, "Frank, take this home to your folks. Happy Thanksgiving." He again became Mom's "knight in shinning armor."

Numerous dogs kept following Frank home and Mom kept them for a while until they either ran away or died some way. I think Frank brought Skeezix the cat home. She stayed a long time. Our mother had an extensive tolerance for helpless people and pets.

A beautiful German shepherd, Jack, entered our lives one Fourth of July as fireworks boomed outside. We had a small entryway into our flat that we never locked at night, and Jack must have given it a slight push and opened it. He was so terrified that he entered the hallway and flopped right down in the corner for safety. That's where we found him, scared to death from the fireworks that we later discovered the kids on the block were tossing at him.

Since he had no identification tags, Mom had us bring him in and feed him. He was really a friendly animal with a gray coat and splashes of brown and white fur. For some reason we named him Jack. Not only did we stroke and love him, but we also stroked and loved Skeezix. They slept together by the potbelly stove in the kitchen every night, with the cat curled up in the center of Jack's body.

Sadly, however, Jack ran off one year later when the fireworks frightened him again. Mom got angry with us for not watching him more closely. And, since he was blind in one eye, we feared that a car hit him. The cat remained but Mom, and especially Daddy, refused to take in any more strays after that.

Chapter 7

Sometime during these years, Uncle Tony and Aunt Grace came into our lives. Uncle Tony was Daddy's youngest brother. They arrived from New Orleans with an air of sophistication. Aunt Grace's expensive clothes and Uncle Tony's educated demeanor impressed us greatly. Everything about Aunt Grace exemplified wealth or bordered on the edge of affluent; her beautifully manicured hair, her fine wools, dangling bracelets, and diamond earrings all defined her and she smelled divine.

As a young and very impressionable girl, I felt completely in awe of her. But mostly, I remember Uncle Tony's laugh. He chuckled softly and expensively and his eyes truly sparkled. Baldness ran in the Zimardo family. All the boys had what we called "the St. Anthony ring." Uncle Tony had it, too, but on him it really looked good.

I remember going to their apartment on the north side of Chicago near the downtown area. After a while, Aunt Grace took Marie by the hand into her bedroom, as I trailed behind, to show us her shoe collection. I can actually see her right now bending down to pull out boxes of shoes. Most were black suede pumps.

"I love to go to Aunt Grace and Uncle Tony's apartment. They have such pretty things," I said to Mom one day.

"Don't get so carried away with her pretty things," answered Mom. She's got a gray side to her."

I thought about Mom's comment, but it took a while before I realized what she meant.

Helen, "Aunt" Grace, and Marie

Marie actually caught on quicker than I did when Aunt Grace began to bring her priest friend, Father Pat, along to our house each time they visited. Marie called him her "drinking buddy." After a few stiff drinks, Grace sat on his lap, kicking her feet up—by this time had lost their shoes—and they'd party. Uncle Tony, being a quiet drinker, didn't seem to mind any of this at all. However, this behavior outraged Daddy and Mom.

I remember one time driving either to their apartment or back to our house, for some reason, and someone had to lap ride—something not permitted today, of course, due to seat belts. I was the most likely candidate due to my size and young age, but Father Pat insisted that Marie sit on his lap. She was close to sixteen at the time. She did reluctantly and regretted doing it, as his hand gently rubbed up and down her back. I teased her about that for months. From then on, Marie spent many hours quietly reading in her room whenever they came over. The visits went on for some time, and probably only because Uncle Tony was my Dad's brother. Daddy always loved to play cards, but even that became strained and uncomfortable for my parents at times. Aunt Grace frustrated everyone when she played the wrong card at the wrong time, giggling in the process. Daddy's patience wore thin.

Finally, because Mom couldn't take it any longer, she began to offer excuses for not getting together. She probably got tired of seeing Aunt Grace inebriated. The priest—well, he staggered after her as they left.

"We have a picnic this weekend, Grace, sorry." Or "The kids have a special program at school this weekend, sorry." Dad's health came in handy once in a while, also. "Jasper has a bronchitis infection, Grace, sorry." Until finally, Grace stopped calling. They always ate well and got treated royally at our home, so it took a while before they got the message.

Our parents had other friends, too. I will never forget the Medford family, or Mr. and Mrs. Newford. Being the last child in the family cuts off my memory bank, but I can say that these friendships probably started when I was quite little, while we lived on Harrison Street. It seemed the Medfords came to our house for years just to play pinochle. Daddy loved the game.

Every Saturday night, the Medfords arrived right after dinner like clockwork. Mom pulled the tablecloth off the dining room table, grabbed pencil, paper and cards from the drawer, and all four sat down to begin. They never even said "Hello." Before the evening ended Daddy, in a fit of temper, usually ordered Mrs. Medford out of the house, claiming vehemently that she cheated. This generally happened every time she trumped his ace. The cards fell a certain way and there was no way she could have cheated, but no one could convince him of that. Mom always tried to calm him. Sometimes the big scene happened right after dessert, or they might not even make it to dessert. Mr. Medford said very little. He just picked up and followed his wife out the door. The following Saturday, she and Mr. Medford arrived at the same time for the same game.

The Medfords had five children. Their oldest girl, a very pretty girl around sixteen or seventeen, caused them many headaches around this time. She generally babysat with the kids when they came to our house to play cards. But one evening, after the police picked her up for stealing and she had to spend the night in jail, Mrs. Medford asked our parents if they could play cards at her house. Nothing stopped the game!

I will never forget standing in front of the county jail looking up at the heavy bars on the window of this huge solemn gray structure as she waved to us down below. Mom, Marie, and I went over before the game to visit her. Only family went indoors, so we stood out on a cold, snowy night waving while Mom's eyes filled with tears.

"Poor Marian," she said over and over.

That same night, we trudged our way back to the Medfords' house in the snow. Marie went in ahead of me while I took off my galoshes. Out of nowhere, the huge dog they generally locked up in the back bedroom escaped. He made a lunge for Marie and nearly bit her leg off. She screamed and I shook from head to toe until they corralled this animal. The dark room filled with old furniture and dim lights turned into bedlam, and this was one time the card game actually ceased.

Daddy and Mom rushed us home. Marie's leg was bloody with teeth marks. Mom applied peroxide immediately and wrapped it with a clean white handkerchief as Marie cried with pain. They never played cards at the Medfords again. Mom made numerous trips back and forth to the doctor with Marie, and it took months for her to heal.

Card games continued at our house with the Medfords, but the young daughter? Well, she turned out just fine. After spending a night in jail, she did a complete turnaround. She graduated from school, then met and married a young man from Alaska. This happened many years ago, and it's quite possible that she still lives there.

ෆ   ෆ   ෆ

The Newfords were a different breed altogether. They didn't live a long time in Chicago, but rather bought a farm in Wisconsin. One bright spring day, probably late April, when a few wildflowers showed their usual pretty faces by sprouting up around the houses on Claremont Street, a knock came to our door.

"I'll get it," said Marie.

Mom followed with "Well, hello, how are you?" Her arms extended, she hugged both Mr. and Mrs. Newford and said, "Come on in" in her never-to-be-lost Louisiana accent. Something about these people always cheered Mom up. They were ordinary people. Mrs. Newford was tall and hefty, with brown hair and a pretty face. Her husband, also tall but slender, bordered on bald and had laugh lines around his gentle eyes. Mom really liked them. They were on their way back to Wisconsin, but she talked them into staying for dinner. Daddy by this time had become a liquor salesman, setting up his own time and deliveries. So he walked into the house just shortly after they arrived.

53

They enjoyed the time together and Mrs. Newford took a liking to Marie and me.

"Why don't you let the girls come home with us? Our family would love to have them. The twins, Eddy and Donald, are about Marie's age and they'll have a good time on the farm," said Mrs. Newford.

Our brothers weren't home, making us the lucky ones to who got invited.

"Oh, you have enough kids of your own," said Mom. "Why would you want a couple more?"

"No, seriously, Augustine. Let them come. The animals will keep them busy."

Mom looked at Daddy. Daddy shrugged, raising his eyebrows indicating why not, and Mom said, "Okay."

Marie and I went home that evening with the Newfords to add to their family of five or six. Marie seemed hesitant, but I was beside myself with excitement. It was the first time we had ever seen a farm and for two weeks we smelled fresh hay, fed chickens and pigs, rode horses, and watched a full moon light up a dark Wisconsin sky. I loved every minute of it. Marie had a couple of homesick nights but generally, we found the whole experience totally heartwarming—and totally different from city life.

The rooster did crow at dawn. For some reason, I never really believed that until I heard him every morning for two weeks. The sun shone its brightest while the smell of freshly brewed coffee seeped its way up through our open window.

Then came the chicken cackling as Mr. Newford walked around strewing chicken feed all along the ground next to the barn. I remember jumping out of bed and running to the window where I could watch the oldest son, Dennis, and twins go into the barn to milk the cows. After we dressed, Marie and I ran to the barn to watch the milking.

One of the twins—perhaps Eddy because he was the practical joker—urged Marie to sit on the stool, promising to teach her how to yank on the udder to fill the milk bucket. But, instead, he lifted the udder in her direction and squirted her in the face with the warm milk as he merrily doubled over with laughter, causing his straight blonde hair to fall down over his eyes. She, cherub-faced with curly brown hair, got angrier by the moment as she wiped milk off her face with her hand. Finally, she picked up a hand full of hay and stuffed it down the back of his shirt and walked out of the barn. I was too young for all of this tomfoolery, but after the many tricks he played on her, even I could see that Eddy was smitten with Marie.

What a healthy, happy bunch they were. I still remember Mrs. Newford's delicious fried chicken, mashed potatoes, pot roast, fresh corn on the cob, and the family favorite dessert, gingerbread cake topped with large portions of fresh whipped cream. We waited anxiously every suppertime for her mouth-watering meals and she never failed us.

The joy of the freedom we found on the farm can't really be explained in words only experienced and recognized. I vividly remember riding free-saddle across the countryside rounding up the cows. Either Donna, the Newfords" oldest daughter, or Eddy always picked me up and sat me in front of them on a favorite horse. I found this scary at first, then glorious. I could be wrong, but somehow I remember Donna's horse's name as Pepper. It very well could have been, since he had a silky, shiny coat with a copper mane and tail. We rode into the wind as we scurried around the cows, trying to corral them back behind the gated fence. Talk about excitement! Nothing can compare.

Some parts weren't always pleasing for two city rascals like us, age eleven and almost fourteen that summer. Feeding the pigs, for instance, wasn't one of our favorite things to do, but we took the good with the bad. Mrs. Newford always made up for it with a special dessert. Slits in an apple pie oozing with cinnamon are my most pleasant memories.

Then it all ended. We lived and relished a dream come true,

wondering if we could ever repeat such an experience again in our lifetime. I don't know if Marie, in her later years, thought about the love and laughter we enjoyed that summer, but I shall never forget it.

The Newfords returned us to our home after a couple of weeks, but we only saw them occasionally after that. We heard years later that Mrs. Newford was very ill with diabetes and partially blind, which broke our hearts to hear since she was such a caring person. Their children grew up and had children, which happened in our family also. But in my memory's heart I wish every child the joy of a farm, even for just two weeks, where love, laughter, good food, and animals fill up a day. Also, I wish every child could experience the bright full moon and the warm breeze that filters into a bedroom window while fresh coffee permeates the air.

Chapter 8

In the years that followed, Mom made many friends on the block. I recall Bea, Rose, Ellen, and Lee, who all lived across the street from us. The adults spent their evenings after dinner visiting on the front porch as the kids played baseball, hopscotch, and hide and seek, or jumped rope or rode bikes. Meanwhile, the grown-ups talked and laughed over day-to-day situations.

With her warm laugh and her storytelling ability, Mom attracted company. Whenever they saw her sitting out, the neighbors wandered over and plopped themselves down on the front stairs. Everyone on the block truly treasured these short-lived summer evenings.

The children from our neighborhood attended one of two schools: King and Precious Blood. Students from the south end of our block went to King and the north end, where the Irish families lived, attended Catholic school. But most children at that time had summers off for freedom, and we all had calendars to scratch off the final days to the last day of school. Then from June on, summer always flew by and the end of August arrived far too soon.

From June to August each year, many things happened that left lasting memories. I can see Rose nursing her baby on the porch bench, covering her breast with a baseball hat, towel, sweater, or whatever she found available. Bea and Ellen lived in the back apartments of a duplex directly across the street from us. They used to wander down the passageway, spot Mom, and come over.

Ellen, a meticulous woman about five-feet-six inches tall, had a loud, deep laugh that would have suited a woman a foot taller. She had finally divorced a man who rarely came home and took a swat at her occasionally. She had two teenage daughters, the oldest of whom Ellen spanked constantly for getting dirty, talking out of turn, or any other annoyances Ellen couldn't stand. When Ellen came over to sit on the front porch, we all gathered around to hear the latest episode.

"I'll brain her yet. She's nothing but trouble." She usually started off talking about Marilyn this way. "She didn't attend school yesterday. I'm tired of the teachers calling me. She's running around with some creep." Or, if poor Marilyn happened to have had one good day, the subject turned to Nick, Ellen's ex-husband.

"The bastard. Because he knows I'm working and making money, he comes over to borrow. My mother said, "If you give him any money, you're nuts.""

Then someone in the group always asked, "Well, did you?"

"Did I what?" she answered.

"Did you give him any money?" came the exasperated question.

"Yeah, anything to get rid of him," Ellen always answered.

To no one's surprise, Nick never paid Ellen back and she continued to hand out.

Ellen usually raved on until Bea strutted out of the passageway and joined the group. Immediately, the subject changed and we'd hear Ellen's boisterous laughter pretending it has all been a joke. Why? Because Bea's patience ran thin when it came to Ellen's problems. The word "strut" seemed very appropriate for Bea. She'd place her hands on her hips, throw out her buxom chest, and peacock-walk across the street. She, too, worked a full-time job and had a teenage daughter to raise, but Bea respected her daughter and got it back in return.

"Ellen," Bea would say, leaning right into her face, "you need to learn how to deal with a teenager. You keep harassing her the way you do, and she's going to run away from you."

And that's exactly what happened. In the winter of 1940, we all watched with sadness as Marilyn went downhill. It was a pity, for even now I can see her freckled face, dark brown hair, and sweet smile as a youngster. She finally couldn't take the verbal and physical abuse any longer from her mother and ran off with "some creep," as her mother liked to say. She had one child, then another, another, and finally a fourth, coming home pregnant between each one.

Ellen helped her with each child and then Marilyn, too, began to abuse her children. The oldest often exhibited bruises on her face and body, which her mother claimed came from falling out of a highchair. One excuse after another followed the constant bruises and cuts each child had, until the baby's arm was broken.

With strong conviction, the neighbors all made the same comments to Ellen: "Take those children away from her." We talked a lot about it at our house as well. Mom served as a sounding board and listened many days to Ellen as her tears flowed with desperation.

Finally, the end came and social workers took the children away from Marilyn. Two went up for adoption and Ellen kept two. Marilyn's sister, Joan, may have taken one of the children after she married. We never quite knew how that turned out, because they left the neighborhood and moved to larger quarters. No note, no goodbye. Just one day they were gone. However, these people form part of the lasting memories of our growing-up times.

CB   CB   CB

Through it all, Mom kept a watchful eye on us, never becoming complacent or careless about the company we kept or the places we wanted to go. She checked and rechecked our friends and we had to report our whereabouts at all times. The only time she freely let us go was when the school nuns took us on trips.

I remember one class trip in September, a generally beautiful month for outings in Chicago. We all enjoyed the early fall breezes, comforting and cool, and could go almost anywhere in a light jacket or sweater, knowing quite well that the blasts of winter were not too far behind.

I brought a note home one day asking for Mom's signature so that our class could visit the county jail for a special project on prisoners. A cool day arose that morning with sprays of sunshine and, of course, we all felt excited about not having to sit in class. The Sisters of Mercy, always so organized, made sure a bus pulled up on time in front of the Church, opened its wide doors, and beckoned us to ascend. Excitement reigned as we ran merrily to our seats. Everybody wanted a window, of course, but Sister Andrew straightened that problem out in a hurry.

"Sit," she said sternly. "Anywhere." And fifty kids all sat at the same time. She was the only one who could do that. A couple of boys tried to outwit her once, and for days they walked around with sore red ears twisted by a determined hand.

Aside from the rows of jail cells that contained one or two men who shared bunk beds, a washbasin, and a toilet, I remember a long, dark dungeon area, perhaps down in a basement known as Death Row. We all trembled slightly because it felt so scary. Seeing the sad, depressed men occupying the cells in the previous rows felt bad enough, but to walk through even a more dissipated corridor of human hopelessness felt like more than we could bear. Why the nuns felt that youngsters of ten and eleven years required such an education not only baffled our parents, but us as well. They probably thought if we youngsters saw the end result of sin, we'd stay away from it. Some logical thinking to that!

Anyway, as we passed a huge iron door with a tiny opening, I heard my name. I was the second to the last student in a long line, so I jerked around thinking the girl behind me called. She had not.

I looked at the opening in the door and a mouth said, "Helen. It's me, Eddy." I shrank and my legs turned to rubber. We had two nuns with us, one who led the pack up front and one who brought up the rear. Sister Theresa, the nun in the rear, heard my name called and pushed us along quickly. Was she worried I'd stand there and carry on a long, friendly conversation with him? I think not. I felt too terrified to speak.

No one said another word about the incident. As a treat we got ice cream cones after the outing, and I kept waiting for Sister Theresa to say something more to me about the death-row prisoner. But apparently from the nuns" point of view, the incident never happened.

When I repeated the story to my family on our return home, my mother only had one comment: "Helen, can you go anywhere and not know somebody?"

We later found out that Eddy was a boy in the neighborhood who had been involved in a murder. I didn't really know him. He knew our family strictly as residents on Claremont Street, and probably knew my brother more than any of us. Now, after all these years, I still prefer to think that Eddy was innocent.

Chapter 9

Early one morning in December of 1941, the pastor of our church and school tapped on the classroom door. A tall man with a masculine build, Father Bird must have been quite handsome in his youth. Now, gray hair surrounded his aging features. Sister Angela Maria stepped off the platform that supported her desk and opened the door. After a few whispers and nods, Father came into our classroom. Twenty-six fifth graders came to attention, instantly quiet. Father's presence was sacred to us.

"Class," said Sister. "Please sit up straight. Father has a message for you." Father Bird slipped into the chair behind the desk and sat there silently. We all shifted our eyes from the multiplication tables Sister so meticulously displayed on the blackboard to the sad face and lined mouth that finally spoke.

"Children, this is a sad day for America. We are at war. The Japanese have bombed Pearl Harbor." Then he pulled down the world map over the blackboard and continued, showing us Pearl Harbor's location. Not really understanding the impact of Father's words, we all felt sad because he seemed so sad. Looking at Sister Angela Marie made us even sadder.

That night, as everyone tuned their radios to our President's speech, we heard him say, "This is a day of infamy." Although our parents said little, we knew Mom and Daddy worried about Frankie and Joe having to fight in a war. This thought caused all of us to slow down and view our daily routine differently. We all put less emphasis on unimportant matters.

Frankie was eighteen at the time, and anxious. It seemed that from the very beginning, he felt destined to join the Marines. Mom, troubled that he might enlist, expressed no surprise when he did.

"Why don't you wait, Frank until you're drafted?" she asked.

But Frankie saw no sense in furthering his career as a civilian if the war eventually forced him to drop everything and go into the service. And so he left junior college, his family, and his girlfriend, Janet, behind him in a fever of patriotic excitement. He attended boot camp at Camp Lejeune, Jacksonville, North Carolina, and we all wrote faithfully. My daily routine included rushing home from school anticipating a letter from Frank.

Mom's devotion to the Sacred Heart grew even stronger during these trying times, and she attended Mass and Communion many mornings after the Marines sent Frankie overseas to Guadalcanal after boot camp.

Shortly before the Japanese bombed Pearl Harbor, Joe and Mary got married. It actually happened the September before, with the reception held at her family's home. They could no longer keep their courtship secret, and finally both families met at an engagement party held at Mary's home. Mary's hard-working Italian family accepted Joe. And eventually, her father accepted us. At first meeting, he felt reluctant to acknowledge Joe as a prospective son-in-law because he wasn't Italian. Joe was Irish and German and still a Dunn—Mom insisted he keep his father's name. But after Mr. Yaconetti met Daddy and found out he was Italian, his thoughts changed and he accepted the marriage.

"Jasper, what part of Italy you from?" he asked.

"My family came from Sicily," Daddy answered.

"Good, very good," he said in his thick Italian dialect.

As a married man, Joe initially got a deferment from serving his country. As the war proceeded and Germany got involved,

63

though, he finally got drafted. Early one morning, tears streaming, we all hugged and kissed Joe as he said goodbye to follow his brother into the Marines. Mary returned home to live with her parents and work full time. Again, Mom invoked the Sacred Heart to watch over her two boys. Joe eventually ended up in Okinawa, Japan, as the heat of the battle there grew severe.

"There I was in a fox hole," he said later. "Tired and dirty, and I got thirsty. I left my buddy sitting next to me and got up to pull my canteen from my belt to get a drink of water. I dropped the cap to the canteen and as I bent over to pick it up, a sniper's bullet flew across right where my head would have been. I am lucky to be here today."

When my mother heard this, she mumbled a short prayer of thanks.

Each day we wrote and prayed. After boot camp, Frank came home on furlough and we celebrated. I had taken over his room in his absence, but cheerfully returned to sharing a bed with Marie or even sleeping on the couch at different times. His homecomings brought on happy times full of fun, as Mom prepared his favorite meals.

World War II also brought the neighborhood closer together. The newspaper began to write stories about the Victory Gardens sprouting up all over the country. Claremont Street, too, decided to do its part and we all assembled to plan one.

Claremont ran south from Flournoy to Taylor Street. A small macaroni shop sat on the west side of Taylor, where residents and passersby popped in to pick up miscellaneous items. Balls of assorted cheeses hung in the window and they considered their freshly made Italian sausage and their still-available imported olive oils their specialties. Searching for a more available spot for their Victory Garden, the neighbors decided to explore the lot on the corner of Claremont and Flournoy, which turned out to be the likely place.

Buddy, the author's husband in World War II

Joe Dunn, the author's half-brother

Frank P. Zimardo, the author's brother

Jack Kedzie, the author's brother-in-law

After a few workers softened and cultivated the hard soil, both groups and individuals strolled down to the corner lot in the early morning sunshine to plant all around the center pole graced by our American flag. People planted varieties of flowers in creative designs as well as herbs, lettuce, tomatoes, radishes, carrots, regular parsley, Italian parsley, and green onions. Of course, rows of hot peppers also ran the length of the huge garden. People took turns watering, and everyone got the opportunity to taste and eat delicious produce that came from a dedicated team of workers.

Claremont pulsed with activity back then, and we felt ourselves at the center of a thriving metropolis. Every day delivery men brought goodies to our streets and alleys ranging from vegetables and fresh fruits to popcorn, taffy apples, pumpkin seeds, and the Good Humor Man. We also got milk delivery and Italian bread from Fontana Bakery down on Oakley and 24th Street. But we also had a small A&P store on Harrison Street where they sold three kinds of Eight-O-Clock coffee in a red bag, Circle in the yellow bag, and Bokar in the black bag. Mom made a special trip to the A&P just for the coffee. We all loved the incredible brewing aroma of coffee in the morning.

But our favorite delivery was the iceman. We'd snitch the pieces of hard, clear ice that he chipped off before hoisting huge blocks with his leather-covered shoulder. Mom always lined the trail from the front door to the icebox with newspapers to catch the drippings. Adding a Victory Garden only enhanced our bustling, thriving neighborhood.

Chapter 10

Before we realized it, Marie graduated from Precious Blood School and headed to St. Patrick's High School. Privately, I felt glad to see her go. As I followed her from grade to grade, each nun graciously reminded me of how much we differed.

"YOU are Marie's sister?" they asked with raised eyebrows and nervous smiles.

For one thing, Marie was much taller, with a lovely face, long, curly brown hair, and gorgeous blue eyes. She was beautiful.

I, on the other hand, stood (and still stand) four feet, nine inches tall, with perfectly straight, dull, colorless blonde hair and a large mouth. Marie and I had only our blue eyes and our last name in common. To my dismay, Mom had my eyes tested when I was in third grade and decided I needed glasses. After seeing myself in our classroom group picture, I gagged. Convincing Mom I didn't need them wasn't easy. Once I proved I had no problem reading without them, she let me stop wearing them. I didn't wear them again until many years later.

Marie was nearsighted and wore glasses constantly from second grade on. But even with glasses, she was beautiful, which probably explained why she got the lead in the eighth grade play put on every year by the school. If I remember rightly, it was called "The Great Stone Doorstep" or something like that. We went as a family to see the show, and Marie amazed us all. Her leading man got more serious than Mom cared to see. But it was all in fun and after they graduated, the boy stopped hanging out at our house, which drew a sigh of relief from our mother.

Before Marie enrolled at St. Patrick's High School, Mom worried quite a bit about the tuition. She wasn't sure we could afford it. However, Marie had become very good friends with two Irish girls on the corner of Claremont, Virginia and Peggy Martin, and wanted to attend the same school. So, coming to her children's rescue as always, Mom talked to the principal of Precious Blood School, who said, "I'll see what I can do." Since Marie was an "A" student, an academic scholarship might be possible. As it turned out, she only received one year of free tuition, but since Daddy worked full time at a tool company now, and Marie loved attending St. Patrick's with her friends, Mom agreed to leave her there in hopes she'd work out the finances somehow. At fourteen, Marie was too young to get a part-time job, since in 1942 students could not get work permits until age sixteen. Baby-sitting jobs in the neighborhood helped out up to a point.

St. Patrick's High School stood on Des Plaines and Adams in the heart of Chicago. Marie's homeroom nun, Sister Olivia, was a hoot—you just had to love her. The Sisters of Charity nuns, an order founded by Mother Seton, ran the St. Patrick's Girls School. The Girls' School faced Des Plaines Street and the Boys School faced Adams. Every day, Marie told us stories about the girls hanging out on the fire escape to clean erasers so they could get the attention of the boys. If Sister Olivia caught them, she made them stay an extra night after school to wash the blackboard down. The girls then took care to wring the rags out on the fire escape. Their teacher pretended she didn't notice.

Sister Olivia was definitely not a disciplinarian. She exemplified everything the Charity Sisters stood for: love, kindness, caring, and compassion. Every Thanksgiving and Christmas, the Order distributed huge baskets of food and boxes of used clothing to the poor, and the girls accompanied the nuns on their journeys. To this day, I remember visiting apartments on second and third floors, with stairways barely clear enough to walk. Dirt and debris collected in corners and runners, if any, were torn and stringy. Graffiti covered the walls and little children sat on porches with running noses and no shoes, immune to the cold and ice—or maybe just too hungry to notice.

While Marie attended high school and I was in seventh grade, the family still called 714 South Claremont Street home, and had done so for quite a long time. As I mentioned earlier, Daddy got a job with a tool and die company called Cinch and finally settled in for a long stay.

CR   CR   CR

During our domestic contentment, the war carried on and a letter came from Aunt Katie. She told our parents that her adopted daughter, Ruth, lived in Chicago now, and felt very much alone because her husband was in service. Could she stay with us for a short while until she found an apartment? Mom, the perpetual softy, always had a hard time saying "No" to salesmen, stray animals, and imposing relatives. The day Ruth arrived, we all wanted to check out. Oriental-looking with slanted eyes and black hair, Ruth had the strangest-looking mouth: some of her front teeth were gold, lined with black. Also, she blew her nose constantly; she had severe allergies and left a trail of snotty tissue wherever she went.

Because Frank was still in service and overseas now, Ruth got his room. I, of course, had to return to sharing the bedroom with Marie again. Ruth settled in immediately. Here was a woman in her middle thirties who stayed up half the night and slept till noon every day. While Mom served lunch to the rest of us, Ruth ate her breakfast in a soiled white terry cloth robe while she coughed and blew her nose. After more than an hour sitting at the table reading the newspaper, she left behind dirty dishes and piles of soiled tissue. We did her laundry, served her meals, and eventually had to clean her room. She had no concept of cleanliness.

Marie could barely tolerate her and complained constantly.

"I can't stand her, Mom. She's disgusting, and what's that terrible odor coming from that room?"

After a period of time, we all began to smell an unusual, pungent odor that seeped through the house. After further questioning, we discovered she was inhaling pot (marijuana) at night. She insisted she smoked it for her allergies.

The day finally came, though, when Mom suggested she look for a job. It took Ruth several weeks before she made the attempt, but to no avail. She insisted, "It's useless. No one is hiring." But with a war on, businesses were looking for people to hire.

Daddy's suggestion: "Why don't you write Katie? Tell her that Ruth is another mouth to feed and we can't afford her."

At first, Mom pooh-poohed the idea. Then, remembering that her sister Katie lived in wealth, health, and comfort, she reconsidered. Drawing the shades and lighting the lamp one evening, she sat down at our dining room table and wrote a letter.

Dear Katie,

Ruth has been with us several months now. She eats and sleeps well and continues to be strong and healthy. Her allergies are a bit annoying to her, but since our Helen seems to have the same problems, we are convinced that the damp spring weather can be somewhat responsible for her condition. Anyway, Helen seems to feel better when she's up and out to school every day. The spring and fall in Chicago are peak allergy times.

Jasper has finally found a secure job, but the expenses of a large family can be overwhelming at times. Ruth has been looking for a job, but so far has not had any luck. The war seems to be winding down and if Frank comes back to his room, we will have to make other arrangements for Ruth in order to keep her here. That may be an added expense.

We hope you are fine and thought it best to keep you informed.

Love, Augustine

One week later, a check came from Aunt Katie for one hundred dollars. It certainly helped with expenses, but it didn't get rid of Ruth. Clearly, Mom had to find another strategy.

Chapter 11

In spite of the havoc that continued in our home over Ruth, life went on with other members. I, for one, moved into eighth grade and began to act on the desire that had lain dormant since birth. Though I didn't realize it myself, the nuns saw signs of writing ability. English, literature, composition, and creative writing became my strong subjects in class, and they assigned me to a brand-new teacher.

Sister Angela Marie, my fifth-grade teacher, had an outstanding background in English. Young and fresh from California, she was sophisticated in her teachings and expectations, showing her preference to the wealthier kids in the class. Our initial relationship didn't go too well.

More than once, I told Mom that Mary Ann was Sister's "pet" because of her expensive clothing and perfectly groomed hair. She demanded perfection and I was anything but. Ink spots easily found their way to my blouse. My hair never looked neat and orderly—it always seemed to just hang there in this dirty-looking color of brown. My mother gave up on doing anything about it a long time ago. Beyond my appearance, my desire to laugh and cut up in class annoyed Sister more than anything. So, without saying any more, you can draw your own conclusions as to how much she liked me.

One day, she accused me of talking out of turn and demanded

I leave the room. I stood out in the hall crying and suddenly decided to just go home. I spent the walk to the corner of Western Avenue and Harrison Street in tears, but by the time I got past the beauty parlor and pool hall on the south side of the street, I had brightened. The barnyard came up and my eye spotted several short sticks strewn in the grass. The long green fence around the barnyard always tempted me, so without hesitation I selected a favorite stick and ran it across the green boards all the way to Claremont Street. I found great solace in the loud clacking noises that resulted.

However, my tears returned when I stood in the kitchen relating the whole story to Mom. With the water running at the kitchen sink and the dishes clanking, as well as something frying on the stove, I wondered if she even heard me.

But to my amazement she turned the water off, dried her hands, and turned to this pathetic child standing there.

"Get your coat back on. We are paying a visit to Sister Angela Marie," she announced as she quickly turned off the fire under the pan.

Now I felt sick with worry. Mom had a thesaurus of words she hadn't even used yet. Sister Angela Marie was about to get swallowed up.

When we returned to Door 10, our room number, Mom opened it and shoved me in.

"Tell her I'd like to see her out here in the hall, NOW," she said.

I relayed the message and went to my seat in class. I can't repeat the conversation between them because Mom never told me. But I heard her tell Daddy in the kitchen that evening that she called Sister Angela Marie not a Sister of Mercy, but a Sister of Money. I do know that Sister Angela Marie came back into the classroom with tears in her eyes, and she turned into my best friend.

God allowed us to continue our friendship in seventh grade,

when I found myself assigned to her homeroom. Her encouragement and detection of my potential and abilities made me soar, and by the time I got to eighth grade and close to graduation, I brought home As and Bs without any trouble. My confidence reached an all-time high, and her influence made me more determined than ever to be a writer.

But sadness soon filled my heart. Sister Angela Marie didn't return to school after the summer vacation. When they announced that she died of a heart attack, my world collapsed. How could a young, vibrant woman of such perfection die? I asked myself this question over and over. It took me a long time to get past this tragedy. Mom consoled me with, "Helen, she had already reached perfection and God called her home." Maybe Mom was right.

But despite the sadness I really enjoyed my eighth grade year, along with all the other students in my class. We knew each other so well, and *boy likes girl* came and went with lots of fun. We had parties at each others" homes, played Spin the Bottle, and attended with spiritual devotion to the Crowning of the Blessed Mother, Holy Thursday, Easter Sunday, and, of course, the Christmas Birth of our Lord.

As the icing on the cake for me in this joyous year, I was selected as Female Student of the Year at our graduation ceremony. A darling fifteen-year-old named Billy Moser, shy and yet loved by all, was selected as Male Student of the Year. We each received a medal as an award, which I have to this day. Sister Andrew later told me that Sister Angela Marie recommended our names when we were in seventh grade, the year before she died.

Chapter 12

When I graduated from elementary school in 1943, Marie was going into her junior year in high school and Frankie was on Guadalcanal, an island in the Pacific fighting. Mary called periodically to read Joe's letters to us and Mom, in turn, filled her ear about the battle the Zimardo household was having with Ruth. But a break in the Ruth episode finally came.

Several steps led up to our top door from the foyer below. We usually left the door at the bottom of the stairs unlocked until we closed our second-floor apartment up for the night. As dusk began to settle in one night around seven o'clock, we heard a loud knock on our top door. Walking through the sitting room, where a dark green couch and potbellied stove reigned, I heard the knock and opened the door. There, to my amazement, stood a good-looking serviceman in an Army uniform carrying a knapsack over his shoulder that hung down to his waist. Displaying a brilliant smile, he said, "Hi, my name is Danny. Is Ruth here?"

My mother came up behind me and encouraged him to come in. At this same moment, Ruth came out of her bedroom, caught sight of the young man, and went down in a dead faint. Cold applications to her forehead finally brought her about and we discovered he was her husband.

"Noooooo," said Marie. "That good-looking guy is her husband?"

Once we recovered from the shock, we welcomed Danny with open arms. We all assumed he would fling Ruth over his shoulder, race for his white horse, and gallop away with her.

No such luck, though. He moved in. They went into that little three-by-five room and stayed there for days, only coming out for bathroom and meals. Daddy was beside himself.

"Augustine, this can't go on," he told my mother one morning as I gulped down hot Cream of Wheat at the kitchen table. "Get them out of here."

Mom left the sink as hot boiling water filled a soapy pan and turned to him. "Maybe I should write Katie again," she said.

That evening, as a tree swaying from a storm knocked against our dining room window, Mom again sat at the round mahogany table and wrote Aunt Katie.

Dear Katie,

There was much excitement and jubilation over the arrival of Ruth's husband, Danny, a few days ago. He is a delightful young man when we get to see him, but it seems they spend a great deal of private time in the bedroom and it appears he might stay.

We can hardly plan on them living here since our resources are limited, but maybe after their honeymoon time is over, we can work out some sort of arrangement.

Hope you're well.

Love, Augustine

No more than a week later, a letter came from Aunt Katie addressed to Ruth. By this time, this handsome young man started coming out of the bedroom. We'd find him in the kitchen talking to Mom or sitting on the back porch, obviously in total confusion about what to do next.

It didn't take long after Aunt Katie's letter arrived for Ruth to announce that she and Danny were going to find an apartment. She informed us they had been looking through the want ads and planned to move out as soon as they located something. A couple of weeks later, Danny found a job that took them to another part of

Chicago and they moved out. Thank God!

We assumed that Aunt Katie sent more money to help the couple along. Though we never knew exactly what happened, we delightedly threw up the window in the room, gave it a complete airing, and cleaned it from stem to stern. I enjoyed returning to my previous quarters—at least until Frankie returned home.

෨   ෨   ෨

Returning to our normal life gave me time to think now about becoming a student at St. Patrick's High School. Admittance required an entrance exam, I knew. Marie took the same exam and went right into the C class, St. Patrick's highest class. Testing always gave me the jitters, so I didn't fare as well. It's called "mental block" nowadays. The results of my exams indicated Classroom B, which didn't make me totally unhappy because the subjects included sewing and creative writing. I really wanted to learn how to sew, as well as further my ability to write.

But, after a month, the nuns decided to move me into Classroom C, which offered subjects such as algebra, geometry, and history. I complained to Sister Flavia, our homeroom teacher, one day.

"Sister, I want to learn how to sew and write," I said one afternoon after class ended.

"What on earth for?" she asked. "A girl with your brains needs something more stimulating than sewing and writing. We just discovered that you aren't a good tester. You will be much happier in Classroom C."

And that was that.

Was I "much happier"? Algebra and geometry were not my forte and it took me a while to manage them, but history became a favorite. As time went on, I took creative writing as an alternate, but sewing was never a choice. I learned how to sew many years later after marriage.

While I adjusted to a new school and new teachers, Marie had landed a part-time job at a lock factory not far from home. She delighted in Ruth's absence and made Mom promise she wouldn't take in any more boarders. Her pals were the Martin girls and she spent a good deal of time down at the Irish end of the block after she finished her homework. Junior year brought on school dances and meeting St. Pat's boys, one of whom found his way to our doorstep quite often.

Vic Venturi was beefy, to say the least. His brawny appearance suited him well and enhanced his personality. In fact, he was adorable. His energy level always operated at high levels, and he liked to expound at great length on how he felt about Marie. But Vic's affection toward shy, distant Marie, often embarrassed her, especially when he put his arm around her. Daddy always left the room when that happened.

"Do you like him?" I asked in the privacy of her room.

"I don't know," she answered. "He's so loud and talks too much."

But he was fun company, so she continued to meet him at the dances and enjoy his wit. Daddy wouldn't let her date yet, so she and her friends went in groups or just congregated on front porches in the neighborhood.

αβ   αβ   αβ

On warm summer evenings after dinner, the residents of Claremont Street enjoyed staying outdoors playing or watching softball games. The older single people enjoyed this as well as the very young. My friends and I liked to play ball in the passageway between twin buildings that faced Claremont Street.

Several of us, boys and girls, gathered after dinner as we did each summer evening to play a game. My closest friend on the block was Eleanor. I called her "El," and we were inseparable.

A woman named Lottie lived in the first-floor apartment

underneath Eleanor. She was Italian, with dark brown hair, in her forties and unmarried. I don't remember ever seeing her smile.

Practically every day, the kids played baseball in the large passageway between the buildings where El and Lottie lived. We liked to bat the ball straight through to the street. There were windows on each side of the passageway, and Lottie always fretted about these windows getting broken. She often screamed at us to stop playing ball there. We thought she was mean and didn't like kids or baseball.

We were horribly afraid of her. To visit El, I had to walk past Lottie's gray, dismal porch and up a long flight of stairs to her apartment. If I happened to see Lottie nearby or out hanging clothes on the small clothesline that draped across the outer railing I shrank with fear, expecting her to attack me.

Coming down El's stairs one day, Lottie ran out of her back door screaming and shaking her finger in our faces. "If you damn kids don't stop playing ball in the passageway, I'm calling the cops," she yelled. We froze! El had the dark complexion of Southern Italians but on that day, so help me, her face turned pure white as we flew down the stairs. Finally, El's mother convinced us to play ball in the street, but it didn't keep Lottie from spying on us.

We saw her curtains part as she watched where we hit or threw the ball. This went on for some time and then one day, the curtains didn't part.

The curtains didn't part for a whole week. Though young, we became concerned about her. Our imaginations ran wild. El's mother reminded us that Lottie had family in Indiana and she was probably visiting with them. We felt something more sinister must have happened. So when El's mother decided to spend a night with her sick sister, we contrived a plan.

I asked my mother if I could sleep overnight at El's house. She agreed. At eleven o'clock that night, we crept down the stairs to peek into Lottie's bedroom window. We noticed the shade on her window pulled down, leaving a slight opening. Eleanor said, "Need a flashlight. Be right back."

"You're not leaving me here alone," I said. Together, we climbed the stairs while she ran into the house for a flashlight.

Returning to the window, El turned the flashlight on and swirled it around. She gasped, "I see a foot!"

"Let me have that," I said, and grabbed the flashlight from her hand. I saw a foot, too, on the floor next to the bedpost. Falling over one another, we shot up the stairs, afraid of pursuit by demons or ghosts.

El's brother arrived home and found us trembling in her bed. We told him what we saw and convinced him that some type of evil had befallen Lottie. With flashlight in hand and doubting us, he checked out our story. After seeing the foot, he called the police. They found Lottie face down by the bed. She had died of a massive heart attack. Her death shocked the neighborhood. She certainly gained our respect, and we never played baseball in the passageway again.

Police sirens and flashing lights woke Mom up that evening. She slipped out of bed and put her tired old robe on to see just what caused the commotion. Daddy slept through anything and everything. When she saw two medical people carrying a body, she flew out the front door. Imagine her surprise when she saw Eleanor, her brother, and me talking to two police officers. Rushing over, she stood dumbfounded as I whispered, "It's okay, Mom. I'll tell you all about it when we get home." Well, it wasn't okay. Mom didn't let me sleep over at anyone's house for a long time after that.

Chapter 13

Mom didn't look too good as she carried a basket of laundry out onto the porch to hang on the clothesline. To her great pleasure, her years of washing heavy blue jeans over the bathtub were over. The wringer washing machine hooked up in the kitchen seemed to make weekly washing a lot easier, but she still languished. We noticed, too, that she napped more often. When she began to lose weight, Daddy insisted she see a doctor. Mom carried some extra weight, mainly around the middle, but being tall and straight always allowed her to present herself in an attractive manner.

Many years earlier, she lost a lot of weight when diagnosed with a goiter. That surgery took a whole year from which to recover, but this seemed different. She felt listless and dropped a few pounds. Nothing to worry about, as she told Daddy.

When the headaches came, she finally decided to make an appointment with Dr. Bergan, just down the street. A warm September breeze encouraged her to stroll over. She caught the doctor nipping and we laughed about it later. Everyone knew that Dr. Bergan loved his bourbon treat in the afternoon. A goodly amount of wild gray hair graced his head, leading us to believe he was a bit over sixty-five, but he always treated his patients graciously and considerately. And he had certainly worked miracles with members of our family before.

A couple of years before, I developed a nasty running ear that itched and pained constantly. After several trips to an ear specialist without a cure, Mom decided to take me to Dr. Bergan.

"Here," he said. "Take this ointment home and put it in twice a day." Two weeks later, itch, pain, and drainage all disappeared, to our amazement. After that, Mom thought her chances with him were as good as with anyone else.

"Come in, Mrs. Zimardo," he said as he donned his white coat. "And how can I help you this afternoon?" She told him her symptoms.

After an examination of her vital signs, he recommended the usual: blood tests, chest x-ray, and cardiogram. Testing and examination revealed a hernia, quite large, that had to come out at once. Since it pressed on her uterus, Dr. Bergan also suggested a hysterectomy. Mom had her surgery in 1944, just one year before the war ended, and we all worried about her. Letters from Frank, inquiring about her, came as often as possible. Mary called us often, then wrote to Joe to update him on her condition. Mom spent ten days in the hospital, and the surgeon insisted we keep a watchful eye on her.

Mom came home weak and haggard looking. Neighbors came over with dinners and desserts to help the family through these trying times. Many weeks went by before her appetite improved and we began to see a slight glow in her face. The sparkle in her eyes took a lot longer to surface. During this time, Marie and I remained housebound after school. Daddy had a week's vacation coming so he spent the days with Mom, while Marie and I grocery shopped and helped Daddy in the kitchen between doing homework. We managed, but it wasn't easy for us and it certainly wasn't easy for Mom.

When she finally recovered completely, visitors from New Orleans arrived. We stood by and watched Mom's happy smile when she saw her nephew, Lawrence, President of the New Orleans Bank. He was Aunt Carrie's son. Mom felt so proud of him. Another time Aunt Theresa, Daddy's sister, came with her daughter, Rose. We also welcomed family from New Orleans or California, where Uncle Joe and Aunt Dot lived, with great enthusiasm. Other members from our extended family came and went, leaving us wondering about where they lived and wishing we could visit them someday.

Gradually, Mom got stronger and our family gathered closer. December of 1945 brought even more happiness when the war ended. Frankie and Joe both came home. So did Leo and Johnny, at the Italian end of the block, and Marty, Mike, and Jerry at the Irish end. How fortunate we felt not to have lost any of our sons, brothers, or husbands in the neighborhood. When summer came, the boys on the street turned the fire hydrant on again and everyone rejoiced.

As soon as Frankie settled back into his old room, he went out and bought a car. His girlfriend, Janet, married someone else while he served overseas, so Frank launched himself back into circulation for the pickings. He had no problem with that particular category, because women found him not only good-looking but comical, witty, and glib. The women all flocked around. Another thing about him—he always brought his friends home. Many card games and laugh sessions went on around our dining room table until late hours, or until Mom walked in winding her alarm clock. Once he got a job, though, it all ended and he conscientiously woke up bright and early every morning. never missing a day of work.

Frankie was my hero. He always called me "Babe"—I can't remember him ever calling me "Helen" as a youngster. Mom adored him, too. There was nothing he wouldn't do for her. A six-pack of beer got her a room painted, sidewalks shoveled, back stairs swept, and so on and so on. And he'd throw in a few funny remarks to make her laugh.

Joe, on the other hand, was more reserved. However, we did notice that after marrying and coming home from the service, he seemed more outgoing and talkative. He loved to tell us about his experiences in the Marines, particularly his time on Okinawa, and the camaraderie with his buddies. He and Frankie often got into lengthy verbal duel sessions—the highlight of our get-togethers—over the government, politicians, the condition of our country, the Catholic Church, or any controversial subject that concerned our nation at the time. Inevitably, their voices soared, swearing began, and the combat ended in, "You don't know what the hell you're talking about!" Thankfully, at the conclusion of the evening they still remained friends, breaking up the argument with jovial laughter. Underneath, they deeply respected one another. The combat never really mattered, only the chase.

Daddy missed out on most of the fun because he couldn't hear any of it. He had signs of losing his hearing after his bout with scarlet fever many years ago. The children got the fever, then Mom did and finally, Daddy. All recovered, but Daddy's hearing was affected. Now, we had to repeat everything we said, and Mom often got exasperated with him. He said "eh?" to everything and most times strained to hear what was going on.

As rain beat against the kitchen window one afternoon, Mom, Frank, and Daddy sat around the kitchen table talking about the day's events. Practically everything discussed had to be repeated to include Daddy.

"Why don't you get him a hearing aid?" asked Frank.

"He probably wouldn't wear it, Frank," answered Mom. "He's toothless because he won't wear his false teeth. Do you think he'll wear a hearing aid?"

"Try him. I'll help you pay for it." Frank remarked.

The next week or so, Mom took Daddy to an ear, nose, and throat doctor. He confirmed that Daddy needed a hearing aid and recommended a place to go. He came home with a pocket version— nothing like we have today. An apparatus went over the back of his ear and a large battery sat in his shirt pocket. I don't remember what she paid for it, but it wasn't cheap. Frank might have helped her with the payments. I'm not sure and it's really not important, because she always found a way to get what her family needed.

At first hand, Daddy felt enthusiastic about his new appliance. His enthusiasm didn't last long, though. He quickly got frustrated and refused to wear it. Most times, he'd forget to change the battery. It turned into a terrible ordeal and we got so tired of hearing Mom yell, "Put your hearing aid in!" and him answering, "Go to Hell!"

As he got older, our father spent his years in a recliner sleeping. He saw little of what happened around him and heard nothing. I wear hearing aids today, having promised myself not to ever let this happen to me. I want to enjoy the sounds around me— not just verbal conversations, but raindrops on the sidewalk, birds chirping, and children's laughter in a park. Poor Daddy missed out on so much.

Chapter 14

After the war, Frank got a job with a company called MacMaster-Carr. It may still be in existence. And he paid Mom board. Between his board and Daddy's steady income, we had a little extra money in the house. This encouraged Mom to take a trip back to New Orleans, something she had wanted to do for years. She decided to take Marie with her and they'd go during the summer months. They left me behind to keep the house in order while Daddy did the cooking.

The first week they were gone, all went well at home. We got letters and calls from New Orleans telling us how much Mom and Marie enjoyed visiting friends and relatives. Our single, thirty-year-old cousin Eddy, smitten with Marie, loved wining and dining her. And Marie, close to eighteen now, enjoyed every minute of it.

"Oh, Helen," she wrote. "You should be here. I had beignets and chicory coffee in the French Market this morning with Eddy. I don't much like chicory coffee, but the beignets were wonderful."

Another time she wrote, "Eddy took me to The Court of Two Sisters and it was fabulous. The food was divine."

I had to laugh. She picked at food here at home, but suddenly it was "divine" with Eddy. Part of me felt happy for her, another part envious. After all, it was 1946 and I was almost sixteen. I found staying home with Daddy and Frankie anything but exciting. While my sister wandered down wide Canal Street, sprayed here and there with gorgeous azaleas, and strolled the French Quarter, full of music and entertainment, I had to wash dishes three times a day, make beds, and clean house.

Since Eddy played the clarinet on the ship that journeyed up and down Lake Ponchartrain, Marie also got to experience the warm evening breezes that floated across the waters and settled on those strolling the deck. She enjoyed it all and anything I missed mentally, she filled me in through letters and verbal descriptions when she returned home. Mom just gave her usual "Hmm," as she listened to all this, knowing quite well that Eddy needed to find someone more his own age. While still on vacation, she let it all go. But when the letters started coming from Eddy to Marie after they returned home, that's when Mom stepped in and discouraged the whole idea.

"He's too old for you," came first.

"He's your cousin!" came next.

And then, "Do you want idiots for children?"

Mom never pulled punches. She just said it like it was.

I felt ever so glad to have them back again. The whole trip lasted about ten days and by that time, Daddy was beginning to get lonesome for Mom. He started coughing again and his spirits seemed low.

Two years later, I went to New Orleans with two friends and stayed at the house of another cousin, a married woman who drove a cleaner's truck for a living. We had to entertain ourselves and had trouble finding our way around. We never achieved the same enjoyment levels that Mom and Marie did. In fact, it was pretty much a disaster. There was no Eddy for me. He got married the year before.

   ☙   ☙   ☙

After graduating with a secretarial background, Marie needed a better job. She found the lock factory depressing. At home, snow gripped the corners of the kitchen windows while we all stoked the stove, adding more coal to keep the place warm. An early morning in December brought us together around the kitchen table for breakfast while Marie held our attention.

"I would like to quit the lock factory, Mom," she said. "I'll never use my secretary skills there."

"Have you got something else in mind?" Mom asked as she poured coffee from the large ten-cup percolator into each cup arranged on the table.

Head hung low, tinkering with the spoon next to her cup, Marie said, "No."

"Maybe I can get you in at MacMaster-Carr, Marie," Frank offered.

We all remembered that he had just recommended Mary, Joe's wife, a couple of weeks ago, and she got hired. Mary was an excellent typist; we knew the company would appreciate her. Marie would be an asset to any company, also, having graduated with high honors from school.

So early the following morning Marie bathed, put her finest outfit on, calmed her curly hair with a few small dabs of Vaseline, and went in for her first interview. She was hired.

After a year of working at MacMaster-Carr, Marie started to attend the Queen of Angels Church dances. Her two closest friends, Virginia and Peggy, said their Aunt Martha suggested the dances. Every Friday evening, they hailed a streetcar at Western Avenue and rode happily to Montrose to have a good time. Even the streetcar conductor soon recognized their glowing faces as they clung to the streetcar pole waiting to pay their fare.

"Get on board, girls," he'd shout. "Are you off to Queen of Angels?"

They'd giggle while searching for empty seats so they could sit together. Later, another friend, Mary, joined them each week.

Although Marie was a good employee and MacMaster-Carr didn't want her to leave, she stayed a very short time. An opportunity presented itself when a friend told her about an opening for a secretary job at a company called Daprato Studios. Easily accessible by bus, the building sat right down the street from St. Patrick's High School. Nervously, Marie applied and was hired. Not long after, she got a promotion to secretary for the administrator and head of the business department.

Three brothers owned Daprato Studios, which specialized in making religious statuary. The brothers brought the most proficient sculptors and designers over from Italy to work for them. The studios created anything from a six-foot statue of the Sacred Heart to an elaborate altar for a cathedral. High-ranking ministers of the Catholic Church arrived frequently, bringing warmth and friendliness to the small company. Marie loved her job. In my eyes, she was successful, and I wanted to be also.

☷   ☷   ☷

While my sister Marie attended dances and worked steadily at Daprato Studios, I enjoyed developing fast friends in high school and relishing the fun of meeting new boy companions. Mostly, however, I wanted a job. I had had my fill of babysitting and wanted something more promising and substantial.

My friend Josie lived down the street and came from a no-nonsense Italian family who didn't believe in teenagers having fun. As soon as she turned sixteen, her family told her to get a job. Since Josie had a set of twin sisters that stayed glued to her from the time she turned twelve, following her everywhere, Josie actually felt relieved to get out and find a job. I liked Josie, and found her easy to talk to.

One day, sitting on her front porch, she handed me a piece of salami and I voiced my concerns for finding a job. "I'll ask where I work," she offered. Josie worked across the street from my house for a small family business that also worked with religious statuary, only on a much smaller scale. The father did the sculpturing, while the sons extended the business and a daughter-in-law painted. Josie helped with the painting of the smaller statues.

That evening, as the neighborhood kids gathered on our front porch as usual, Josie walked down to tell me that Leo, one of the brothers at the statuary company, wanted to talk to me.

"Come over after school tomorrow," she said.

"Mom, Josie can get me a job across the street at the Cavellis' place. Can I work there?" I asked.

Mom always reminded us of our school work and grades before we attempted another challenge, so I wasn't surprised when she asked, "How about your school work?"

As I bent down to pick up a spoon that had slipped from the table to the floor, I remarked, "You saw my report card. My grades are good."

I had learned to love algebra, but hated geometry. The "C" in geometry didn't help, but since it was the only "C," she agreed on the condition that I improve that grade. I gave her a hug as she ran Daddy's underwear through the wringer on the washing machine.

The interview—my first—scared me stiff. I flew up the stairs of our flat after school and pulled an outfit from the closet, since I refused to go to the interview in my school uniform. Mom had renovated Marie's old uniform to fit me: faded navy with saggy, worn front pockets attached to a jumper. We wore them over white blouses and then put short navy jackets over the blouses. They looked so unattractive.

Hurriedly I dressed, combed my hair, and pinched my cheeks. I didn't wear much makeup at that time. I always had a rather pale face, so pinching my cheeks helped. Then I ran across the street to the back of the Cavellis' house. The door stood slightly ajar, so I slowly walked in. I saw Josie at a long, paint-spattered table, sitting with her back to me. She was painting a miniature statue of the Blue Boy, while the woman next to her painted the eyebrows, eyes, and mouth on a row of statues lined up in front of her. It all looked fascinating. I wanted to work here.

I could hear the loud machine in the back of the shop that sprayed the taller statues with a white base paint. Mr. Cavelli handled the machine, and was covered with white. He smiled when he saw me at the door and lifted his head to his son, indicating my presence to him. Leo turned toward me, holding a statue in one hand and a brush in the other. He was young, perhaps his late twenties or early thirties, and good-looking. The radio blasted a ballgame.

Josie turned around and smiled when she saw me. She mouthed "Good luck" to me.

Of course, we all knew the Cavellis on the block. They had been residents for years. However, the relationship remained casual—hello and goodbye with no opportunity to know them better.

"You come highly recommended," Leo said as he flipped back his light brown straight hair that got unruly and settled on his forehead. He stretched one long leg out before him on a small stool pushed under a desk and said, "If Josie okays you, then we okay you, too. We don't pay a lot. How's fifty cents an hour?"

I didn't hesitate. "I'll take it," I answered

"Fine," he said. "Come in after school and you can have the same hours Josie does. She will help train you. Sometimes, if we have a big order, we'll work later than six o'clock. Would that be a problem for you?"

"No." I answered positively without hesitation, knowing quite well that Mom might not like the idea. When he shook my hand, I felt we had a contract.

I found Mom in the kitchen starting supper. I watched as she added onion rings to the browned pork chops in a cast-iron skillet. The overwhelming aroma of the garlic and seasonings as they blended together was almost more than I could bear. Mom always let us taste, so I waited with bated breath for that slice of bread dipped into the drippings. Oh, my, how great that tasted. She added a half glass of water, covered the pan, and left it to simmer. We loved that meal—it always had side dishes of mashed potatoes and green peas.

As I munched, I talked. "Mom, Leo Cavelli hired me. I can start tomorrow. Fifty cents an hour. What you think?"

"Every day after school?" she asked.

"And all day on Saturdays. Wow, I'll be rich." I swung around. My flared skirt ballooned out around me as I jammed a piece of gravy-soaked bread into my mouth.

"Okay, but remember our agreement. You've got to keep the grades up." Mom smiled, knowing how much the job meant to me.

"Will do," I answered. And I did! My geometry grade improved to a "B" and "As" dominated. Most of all I loved the extra money. I gave Mom five dollars a week and saved the rest. I had little or no out-of-pocket expenses, since I took my lunch every day to school and just bought a soda occasionally. I loved to see my savings increase, but always kept a little on the side for a frozen banana our Good Humor Man brought by regularly.

I enjoyed many happy times as a teenager, but surely working for the Cavellis represented my finest hour. Working each day after school and all day on Saturdays not only taught me how to manage money, but how to attain perfection. The statues had to be totally dry before we touched them and painted carefully, without waste. After we applied color, they sat overnight before we could paint on the faces. Joan, the Cavellis" daughter-in-law and Al's wife, did that job, but she also inspected each statue very carefully for flaws. Each afternoon when Josie and I came in from school, we found our flaws lined up at our station. Joan pointed out our mistakes, and Mr. Cavelli sprayed them again with white paint. After that, we repainted them.

We never heard an ugly word there. Only laughter and polite consideration for each other existed in the back room of this business. When Joan got pregnant, we all pitched in to help her wherever we could. Though we could never duplicate her delicate ability to apply magnificently alive faces on the statues, we offered to help in other ways.

Jokes and wisecracks flew back and forth constantly between Leo and his brother, Al, which kept us bent over in laughter while the radio blared sometimes soft music, other times the Cubs baseball game. We howled when Bill Nickelson got a home run, or Peanuts Lowry stole second base. Phil Cavaretta's double with the bases loaded sent Jack Brickhouse into seventh heaven with "hey, hey." We never really forget memories like these, but store them in our hearts.

I worked for the Cavelli family until I graduated from high school. To my great satisfaction, they offered me a raise to seventy-five cents an hour in my senior year. And then Mom did something we were all hoping for. She called Illinois Bell and had a phone installed. I'd like to think my five dollars a week initiated that. However, Frankie could have proffered to pay the bill, Or even Marie. They both had good jobs and could easily help out.

The excitement began when we put a small table under a window in the hall and the serviceman made the connection. For the life of me, I can't remember the number now. With two single people and a teenager in the house, it rang often.

Josie and I became good friends away from work, also. She lived on a second floor in one of the twin buildings. I remember running up the stairs one day and stopping cold at the opened door that looked into the kitchen. Her father sat at the kitchen table. picking at the head of a cooked calf head that stared at him from hollow eyes. As my stomach turned, Josie yelled, "Bye, Mom." She swung me around to leave and dragged me down the stairs. She obviously didn't want me to see that, but the memory stayed with me a long time. Josie never mentioned this incident, and I never went springing up those stairs again.

From then on, "I'll meet you downstairs on the porch, Josie," became my standard response when we decided to get together.

Chapter 15

Marie, close to twenty years old by now, still attended the dances at Queen of Angels Church. Her friend Virginia had met a Bob, and their interest in one another was developing. Peggy met and married a police officer, while Mary and Marie continued on for the enjoyment of it all. One evening a young man with a sweet smile stood before Marie as she sipped a Coke. Her soft brown hair curled around her shoulders as she leaned against a pole. She looked over her glasses as the Coke ran up and down her straw.

"Would you like to dance?" the young man asked.

"Not right now," she answered. "I'm having a Coke."

"Do you mind if I join you?" he asked. With that, he walked over to the refreshment stand and returned with a Coke. His curly brown hair flopped a bit over his forehead.

"My name is Jack," he said. "What's yours?"

Week after week, they met. With her long black hair and deep dark eyes, Mary attracted a tall, good-looking redhead covered with freckles; amazingly, he knew Jack from attending Lane Tech. Jack had a small car and all four dated regularly. At times, Virginia and her Bob joined them and six people crowded into the small coupe.

Jack Kedzie lived in the Pulaski and Irving Park neighborhood and was Mrs. Kedzie's youngest son. He had a sister named Marie and a brother named Frank, and Frank's wife's name was Helen.

How ironic that the same names turned up in that household as in ours. Further proof that marriages are made in heaven. Jack's dad passed on after a massive heart attack when Jack was a youngster.

Marie and Mary before either married

Around the time she met Jack, Marie also dated a couple of fellows from Daprato. One Larry, in particular, was very interested, but Marie kept them both at arm's length. "Only dates," she told them. But with Jack gaining ground, Mom started to get nervous. At first, the two met at Queen of Angels, but after a while Jack began to come around the house for frequent visits. Jack didn't have a steady job, and this bothered Mom. It may have bothered Marie, also. When I crawled into bed next to her one evening, she told me, "He asked me to marry him, but I don't know." They had been dating a couple of years now, and the girlfriends she hopped the streetcars with to Queen of Angels dances had all gotten married and moved away.

Mom didn't approve of Jack at all. She could see no future or promise in him. She had great expectations for Marie. More than once, she told me, "She's a smart girl and needs an educated man." But what Mom thought didn't bother Jack. He continued his pursuit. He made sure Marie met his family, and they loved her.

ↂ　　　　　　ↂ　　　　　　ↂ

At the same time that Marie struggled with her apprehensions and tried desperately to silence her mother about Jack, Frankie enjoyed forming friendships and playing the field. After a while we barely noticed all the young ladies who came and went through our doorway, because Frank never seemed very serious about any of them. He'd show us photos of beach parties, good times, and hilarious antics, but never focused on just one girl. In fact, Mom and Daddy got tired of meeting the steady parade of girls, because as I mentioned earlier, Frank always brought his friends home and he attracted girls instantly.

One evening though, a certain young lady came through our doorway and we watched as Frank said, "Mom, Dad, this is Florence." The first thing we noticed was her long, shiny black hair that floated below her waistline. Florence was very pretty. She had smooth, delicate olive skin, and wore elegant clothes. I remember the long pearl necklace that adorned the front of a long-sleeved black dress and the ruby-red lips that smiled. Somehow, we knew Frank's search was over. He treated the other girls as casual friends. This one was different.

Dishes clanked on Sunday morning as Mom went through the cupboard to assemble her best china. Marie dressed a beef roast in the kitchen as Mom flipped a newly ironed cloth over the dining room table. Dressed for early Mass, I discovered all this energy going on in the kitchen as I descended the last stair and walked down the hall.

"What's going on? I asked.

"Frank is bringing Florence over for dinner," Marie answered.

Marie handed me a piece of Italian bread that I cheerfully dipped into the beef stock. While I chewed, I asked, "Where'd he meet her anyway?"

At that precise moment, Mom walked into the kitchen and said, "At a dance. He said something about the Continental Hotel."

From the first dinner with Florence, we graduated to evenings and afternoons with Lynn, Marian, and Elaine, all friends of Florence's and really fun and congenial people. We all assumed that this time Frank was serious and a wedding was on the way.

Nothing stayed a secret with Mom. If she had something on her mind, she brought it out into the open. So while we discussed the probabilities and possibilities of Marie's courtship and Frankie's new-found girlfriend, the phone rang. Marie and I usually made a lunge for it, but on this early summer morning in July, 1947, we were slow on the uptake.

Mom answered and we heard her say, "Oh, Mary, that's wonderful. How are you feeling?"

Our heads turned quickly and Marie and I glared at one another when we heard Mom say, "How are you feeling?" Our mother's glow and tender smile told us the news. Mary was pregnant.

Both Joe and Mary, working and scrimping to put money away for a home, did not anticipate a pregnancy yet. They still lived with her family. It was not a good arrangement, with entirely too many people in one apartment. Mary's father was a butcher and her three sisters ranged in ages from middle twenties to eighteen or nineteen. The strict rules and regulations that surrounded the girls created much struggle and tension in the family; they had to sneak to have a personal life, much as Mary did, because of the father's dominance. The mother was understanding and more lenient, but the father dominated her, too. Mary and Joe hoped to leave this crowded, chaotic life behind them soon.

In spite of the turmoil, Joe never complained to us. Some of the episodes at our house between Mary and Mom when they were first married bothered Joe terribly, but he always avoided conflict and stifled his thoughts. Despite his limited education, he was a genius at his job. He took some night courses and excelled, often amazing high-ranking officers of the company who came to him for advice on measurement and design. He had inherited Grandpa Eiler's brain and his father's patience. His deep love for Mary was solid and unquestionable, and no conditions or circumstances could change that.

The thought of the first grandchild in the family exhilarated us. Mary, on the other hand, suffered the morning sickness and queasiness that made her wonder if it was all worthwhile. But nothing stopped her, and each morning she rode the streetcar to work to type her day away and anticipate the arrival of her first child. Mom, the typical grandmother, began buying supplies.

"She will need diapers, blankets, bottles. All sorts of things." That's all Mom thought about. And if you reminded her that this baby was going to take nine months to get here, she'd pooh-pooh you. Thomas Dale Dunn was born May 21, 1948.

In fact, Mom got so preoccupied with the arrival of this child that she remained unaware of the growing relationship between

100

Jack and Marie. They knew they loved each other, and left the future to take care of itself. They planned a September wedding. Fortunately, Jack's prospects seemed more promising now. He had a job, but it seemed obvious that Jack would always work as a laborer. With some training, he could be an excellent electrician or carpenter. Together, they saved. Mom had no choice but to accept and we planned a wedding.

Marie and Jack Kedzie on their wedding day

As the years roll through my mind, I see a photograph of a wedding group glowing in happiness. She, all in white with a shy smile and he, scared but determined to be the best he can be for her. Family and friends surrounded them. Mary Minerva, a true neighborhood friend who came into her life after graduation, stood next to her as her maid of-honor, while Frankie took on the role of best man. Father Jerome blessed them both at Precious Blood Church and the image of their stroll down the aisle is fixed in my mind and will last forever.

We had to admit that Mom did a splendid job helping the couple get off to a good start—she supervised the bridal shower, the wedding reception, and Daddy. Daddy promised he'd wear his hearing aid and false teeth. We saw the pride in his eyes as he gave away his first daughter. I couldn't wait until my own day came. I fantasized walking down that aisle, not realizing how long that would take: I was eighteen at the time and didn't get married until age twenty-six.

Then moving furniture and rearranging our home began. Marie and Jack moved in and everyone got a bedroom, except me. I slept on the couch in the sitting room where the potbellied stove dominated. Everyone told me this was temporary—Frank and Florence planned a wedding the following year, and then I could have Frankie's room again. Eventually, this happened. But the going wasn't always smooth, for many times Mom and Jack locked horns over the matter of Marie and Jack moving out on their own.

I can remember Frank's voice, clear as a bell, telling Mom, "Stay out of it. They're married now. It's none of your business what they do."

But Mom, always headstrong, convinced Marie they could never make it successfully on their own. When Marie announced her pregnancy in February of 1949, Mom emphasized her dependence and need for the family even more. They stayed longer.

Marie was five months pregnant when Frank and Florence got married in July of 1949, and constantly ill. She vomited every morning and gagged all day. The smell of smoke, coffee, toothpaste, and more upset her stomach. She didn't have much of an appetite, and Mom worried about her. By the time Frank and Florence got married, Marie's quirky, queasy stomach seemed calmer and we all hoped for a normal pregnancy for her. As I reflect back, the stress of Mom and Jack's relationship might have caused the erratic pregnancies Marie had with each child.

Frank and Florence had a lovely wedding. I guess you'd call it a "garden wedding." We all wore beautiful pink ankle-length dresses with large straw hats that tied under the chin, and carried baskets of flowers. After they returned from their honeymoon, the couple moved into an apartment in Florence's neighborhood near Chicago Avenue and Spaulding.

Chapter 16

By the time I turned nineteen I dated, but not seriously. I had lots of boyfriends and Daddy complained about getting up out of his chair to shake hands that often. Having graduated from St. Patrick's the year before, through Marie's recommendation I got a job as a stenographer at Daprato Studios. I hated leaving the Cavellis and the statuary business, but they couldn't offer me a full-time job there.

The night of graduation, I sat in an old chair Mom had put on the back porch, smoking a cigarette. Everyone in our family smoked, even Mom. She didn't start until she joined a circle of friends in the neighborhood who liked to meet in the middle of the afternoon just to chat and have coffee. Sometimes they played cards. The women all lit up cigarettes, so she did too. Daddy didn't like the idea at first, but he never could stop Mom from doing anything once she made up her mind. Daddy smoked heavily at the time, too, which contributed to his constant coughing.

I did a lot of sneaking around with my smoking habit, so since everyone had gone to bed and I couldn't sleep from the excitement of graduation, I found solace in the back porch on a clear, breezy evening in June. Remember, I had won the Female Top Student of the Year Award, so I felt pretty electrified by the whole event. I had changed into some lounge apparel and sat there puffing away when Frankie came out on the porch.

"Hey," he said. "Babe, when did you start smoking?"

Sheepishly, I said, "Only this year. All my senior friends did, so I tried it, too."

I didn't bother telling him about the coughing and gagging I did every morning learning how to inhale.

In fact, my friends and I liked to gather at the corner drugstore a block away from school. We'd drink Cokes and smoke away. As I think about that, more girls smoked than the boys, but it made us feel sophisticated. "Cool" wasn't a word in our vocabulary at that time. Little did we know about the fatal outcome of such a habit.

After Frank got over the initial shock of seeing me smoking, he asked, "Well, what are you going to do with your life now?"

I got up out of my chair, walked to the porch banister, and flipped the cigarette over. He, in the meantime, lit one. Turning to face him, I said seriously, "I'd like to go to college. I've mentioned it to Mom and she doesn't think it's necessary, since I've got my secretarial background. Frankie, I really would like more."

"Well, go," he said.

"Mom said we can't afford it."

"Well, I'll help pay for it."

That never happened. However, Mom felt convinced that I would do just fine with my secretarial knowledge. Maybe she was right. But looking back, with more determination to pursue a higher education, a happier person might have evolved. After a while, I felt contented enough with shorthand and typing and the idea of college soon vanished. I have no one but myself to blame, looking back, for with enough determination I could have attended night school.

Daprato Studios was a good place to start in the working world. I found the friendliness of the people and the security of Marie working there up until the time she delivered her baby comforting. I started out filing and eventually became an extra stenographer who took shorthand from the sales representatives.

I remember happy days here, too. Like the time I substituted for Marie while she knelt and held her hands in position to be copied for Father Flynn's statue. Father Flynn needed a model for a six-foot statue of the Blessed Mother he had created. Mary's hands had to have palms together praying and he asked Marie to model for him. I took the shorthand and typed her letters while she knelt in a studio upstairs for days in a very tiring position. My first taste of confidence in a new life.

I also remember Mr. Greco, the head bookkeeper who loved to shop. Short, round, and full of energy, he came back after every lunch hour carrying bags of produce: green peppers, yellow peppers, red peppers, dandelions, apples, huge tomatoes, and always tons of parsley hanging out of a bag dragging behind him. He could swing around the corner of Marie's station light as a feather and rush into his office. He only had sight in one eye and his black hair sometimes hung over the other one, but he could clear that corner wall without any problem.

He had an associate, Billy, a young college student who manned the department in Mr. Greco's absence. Sometimes his boss stayed away longer than an hour. But, Mr. Greco had worked there since the company's launching and, we imagined, the administrators closed one eye as he went by.

I also remember Tommy our mail boy, Leo in the warehouse, Elsie our receptionist, and Jean, who ate lunch with me in a back room scarcely big enough to hold a table and chairs, where we split in two with laughter as she taught me how to knit. If the lunchroom was filled, we'd go into a small one-stall bathroom and lean against the wall as needles clicked and stitches dropped. I am forever grateful for her patience as I watch my grandchildren sleep with blankets, caps, and booties I have knitted over the years. Not to mention the dozens of argyle socks knitted during World War II for my brothers and friend's brothers.

Memories do come stronger the deeper we reflect. I can still recall Marie's hands posed for Our Blessed Mother as she began to moan with pain. Father wasn't quite sure of the sound. At first, he might have even thought it came from the statue until he saw Marie's face turn a funny green shade as she knelt in front of a bench, trying desperately to keep her elbows on the pillow and hands clasped together. As she dipped a bit, he ran around the bench and caught her before she hit the floor.

As a November sky suggested snow, Mom donned her heavy coat, scarf, and gloves to grocery shop before the weather turned bad. The phone sounded as she started out the door. She turned, walked across the sitting room into the hall, and picked up the receiver.

"Hello," she said.

"Mom!" an excited Jack said. "We're at Presbyterian-St. Luke's Hospital. Marie's in labor."

"Oh dear," she said. How's she doing?"

"Not too good. The doctor's thinking about sending her home. She may not be quite ready. He called it "false labor.""

I sat at Marie's desk in front of her typewriter as I waited to hear some news.

Finally, I called home. Marie was sent home from the hospital a couple of hours later after Jack's call

ೞ   ೞ   ೞ

By the unanimous consensus of the family that evening, Marie had to get up off her knees and quit her job. The Virgin's hands would have to wait. Since they were close to finishing the statue, she decided to call Father Flynn.

"Father Flynn, this is Marie Kedzie. I'm so sorry to tell you I can't continue with Mother Mary's hands. But, I'd like to recommend Jean. She has just the slender type of fingers you're looking for and I truly believe that you will be pleased with her. In fact, you will probably find her hands even more appropriate than mine. I'm so sorry."

The following work day, they summoned Jean up to the

studio. One month later, a glowing Father Flynn announced the completion of his statue. Jean took two days off of work to recover from the kneeling position that caused her to bend over in pain.

Mom made decisions quickly and she decided that now, more than ever, Jack and Marie could not move out to live on their own precarious finances on Jack's salary, especially with a new baby coming. Finding Marie napping one afternoon, Mom collected her thoughts and arranged her words in order for Daddy to hear. But, to no avail.

"We'll have to help them, Jasper, with the new baby coming," she said methodically.

"Eh? Who's coming?" he answered.

"Damn it, Jasper. If you don't put that hearing aid in, I'm going to murder you. Your daughter, Marie! She's having a baby!"

"Oh, I know that," he answered.

Putting her hand to her bent-down head, she asked herself, Should I go on?

Finally, after a frustrating struggle, he understood most of it. Tears filled Marie's eyes as she repeated it all to me while we did the evening dishes.

"Do they think loud voices can't get through bedroom doors?" she asked.

"She has us on the poverty list! We have saved for our baby, and Jack's thinking about taking a second job. We don't expect to live here for nothing."

As sarcasm and insinuations crept into remarks or even long stretches of silence bored down, nothing or no one could keep a big, healthy boy from entering this world. We felt slap-happy with excitement. But the delivery wasn't easy. Marie's contractions began again, but this time stronger. Jack ran around looking for his pants and shoes at midnight as she slipped out of bed holding a voluminous stomach. Mom shook me.

"Helen, Helen, wake up. Marie's in labor." she said.

Coming out of my bedroom half asleep and scratching, I

spotted my bundled-up sister waddling like a duck. Jack supported her gently but firmly as they descended the stairs to the ground-floor foyer out into the cold night. Daddy slept through it all. No one felt like yelling in his ear to tell him the news—Mom would pass the news on to him in the morning. And then we waited. Calls came in from Florence, four months pregnant, and Mary, who had her hands full with a one-year-old.

We continued to wait. Jack telephoned periodically to say the same thing over and over, "No, not yet." We all felt sick with worry. We stormed the Sacred Heart of Jesus and his Blessed Mother with prayers. I arose very early to attend Mass and Communion on the second whole day, and finally after a near-death possibility for either the mother or the child, Philip John Kedzie, over eight pounds, was born on November 23, 1949, only through the grace of a loving Lord and the hands of a magnificent doctor.

We rejoiced at the sight of this beautiful little boy with a head full of brown, curly hair. With noses pressed to the glass of the nursery, we watched the sleeping eyes and tiny mouth that moved and twitched. His angelic little face with rosy cheeks bore a remarkable resemblance to his mother.

However, the little angel cried a lot while his mother struggled desperately to return to health. Philip set the whole household into an uproar with his steady crying. Nothing seemed to satisfy him, and he was constantly hungry. Mother's milk wasn't enough, so we switched to bottles and changed formulas continuously. The pediatrician didn't believe in feeding babies whole food until three months old and frequent calls to him only got the same answer: "Let him cry. He's not hungry. Hungry babies sleep a lot."

The tension in our home reached a breaking point, and Mom decided at last to defy the doctor. We bless the morning that Mom mixed up a little Pablum. She placed tiny teaspoon drops of the precious morsel on a silver spoon, and we all glowed as Philip's little tongue slurped up the victuals. For the first time since birth, he slept for four solid hours. The excruciating nights of waking up every two hours ended at last. Every morning and every evening, we gave Baby Phil two teaspoons of Pablum with his bottle and peace once again reigned.

I chuckled on my way down the front stairs one afternoon as I heard Mom talking to her neighbor, Lee.

"This is a big kid. That doctor should have known better."

Chapter 17

It became obvious to all of us that the addition of a new baby meant the need for larger quarters. So when Mom found out at her neighborhood social club that her friend Lee was putting her house up for sale, she began to think. Lee had one of the best-looking houses on the block, always beautifully maintained. They always trimmed the shrubs and applied fresh paint regularly. The two-story yellow brick house faced Claremont Street with an air of sophistication, with several steps leading up to the front porch and wrought-iron railings on each side. The attractive front door had side glass windows, and a short wrought-iron fence circled the yard that Lee's Italian husband, Paulie, mowed and manicured often. A bench sat on the porch waiting for smiling faces and children's laughter.

When Mom presented the possibility, Marie, considered the whole idea slowly and finally spoke.

"Now that Jack's working at Cinch and we are in a better financial position, maybe we can do this." Daddy helped Jack get the job.

With the bit of savings Mom and Daddy felt willing to contribute, we all moved across the street into the yellow brick two-story on a contract that satisfied both families, and an agreement that Mom and Daddy would be paid back over a period of time. It took longer than they anticipated, so you can imagine life being difficult at times during the wait.

Before the move, the whole family took a tour of Lee's house. The long hall from the front door to the kitchen passed a staircase on the right that led up to bedrooms and an upstairs bath. To the left of the hall, a parlor extended into a relatively good-sized dining room, and another doorway led into the kitchen. We all brightened when we saw the screened-in porch and a fenced-in back yard. Daddy delighted in the full basement, and Mom envisioned the ease of hanging clothes there in the winter. It all seemed too good to be true.

Looking back, maybe the young parents should have chosen to go off on their own at this point. Jack and Marie wanted a home of their own, seeking privacy away from a meddling parent. Oh yes, Mom meddled in their affairs. Everyone would have been better off if she saw and heard less. Her interference in Philip's upbringing created havoc because Mom's strong will overpowered parent rules. "Grandma said I can do it!" was Philip's frequent answer from the time he could walk and talk. Marie felt frustrated, especially when Phil slipped into the twos and threes when discipline matters so much. Jack rebelled often and doors slammed, but nothing much came of it.

But when moving day came, the separation issue faded into the background and the whole family moved across the street together. It was a good move and gave all of us a satisfaction knowing we weren't renters anymore. Finally, we had a home of our own. Nothing else changed that much. The same cars parked on each side of the street, and the same vendors and ice cream trucks still descended on us weekly. "Hi Mike, three frozen bananas today, okay?" Baseball games continued to fill our streets. Summers still saw an open hydrant cooling off the block with different kids and winters blew cold winds from the north side of the street to the south. Baseball then gave way to hockey as the kids donned their winter apparel to slide on icy streets pushing a puck. The only big difference was our address, which changed from 714 South Claremont to 729 South Claremont.

We quickly adjusted to our new home. We soon started to talk about putting in a second bathroom downstairs, maybe in the basement, and even considered knocking out a kitchen closet. It didn't have to be a full bath; more like a powder room. We all got a little tired of running up and down the stairs every time we needed to use the toilet.

Augustine and grandchildren Cheryl, Jamie, and Philip, 1954.

As we contemplated this change, Philip finally abandoned the terrible twos, and tired of exploring the pots and pans in the kitchen or lifting ashtrays from one table to another. Oh, he still ran with force when he heard the Lucky Strike commercial on television. He'd dance and twirl as we all clapped, but touch and explore was coming to an end. Captain Kangaroo and Howdy Doody got all his attention now. The day the television entered into the house, our exhilaration with it surpassed anything and everything. We couldn't get enough of it. I heard Mom say the day she shopped for it, "Jasper, we need to keep up with progress. I'm going to look over the televisions in the stores today. Do you want to come along?"

"Where you going?" he asked.

"Probably Sears," she answered

Daddy donned his cap and button-down-the-front sweater. Together, they walked to a Sears store on the corner of Harrison and Western, just short of Precious Blood School, where thirteen-inch televisions were on display.

"I'll take it," Mom said. Our whole living room, as well as our world, brightened when we turned on the set for the first time. Milton Berle helped us forget our troubles with his crazy antics in black and white. So many more great shows followed, making it one of the greatest inventions ever, in our opinion.

We continued to enjoy our new home and another year slipped by. Mary and Joe surprised us all by buying a new home in Westchester, and a sweet little girl was born April 3, 1950, to Frank and Florence. They named her Cheryl. And when they welcomed another little girl born in the same month two years later, in April 1952, they called her Jamie. In four years four grandchildren had come into the family, and the same welcome and excitement encircled each and every one of them.

During this time, Marie dabbled with the idea of going to work again. Frank began his own company as an insurance broker and he hired her to do his secretarial work. Jack now worked with Daddy at Cinch Manufacturing Company and our lives sailed on smooth waters for a little while. However, it couldn't last. Mom found Philip a handful and Marie, leaving the house every morning got more and more difficult.

One morning, exactly a week before her birthday on March 28th, Marie started down the stairs to hurry out the front door for work. Her heel caught the top stair and sent her tumbling all the way down to the bottom. The fall bruised her badly, and the bottom stair jammed against her spine. Luckily, a visit to the doctor determined just bruises, nothing broken, but the decision still loomed as to whether she should continue to work. Mom hassled her constantly about working. Deciding the stress wasn't worth the extra money, Marie quit. Not more than two months later, she was pregnant again.

Mary, too, tried taking on extra work as Tommy got older, but after her Mom and our Mom had put so much time into raising their families, their patience ran thin when it came to handling grandchildren full time.

I don't know about Tom, but Philip never came down with casual colds. When he got infections, they were full blown. He often ran high fevers, and at times fell right into convulsions because of his soaring temperature. We all had the same pediatrician for our children, Dr. Harrison. Marie kept him in business with Phil's constant sicknesses through the winter months, and sometimes even the spring and fall of the year when allergies were so prevalent.

Chapter 18

At age twenty-one, after many friends and casual boyfriends, I wanted more out of my life than being a general stenographer at Daprato Studios. My friend, Eleanor, was married and pregnant. We had shared our teenage years together and attended dances at different ballrooms, eventually making The Paradise our favorite place to meet friends on a regular basis. In fact, Eleanor married Louie, one of the regulars there with whom we shared good times.

But now those years had faded away, and I wanted the security of a home and children of my own. So without the slightest hesitation, I walked into Mr. Byrne's office and quit my job early one afternoon. Mom felt somewhat dubious about my sudden decision, but I convinced her that I wanted more opportunity to meet people of my age. A larger company would be more favorable, I decided, and Mom recommended an employment agency.

After a few interviews, my life changed when the agency sent me to Natural Gas Pipeline Company of America on Wacker Drive. At first, I wasn't too sure. I was hired as Mr. Stubblefield's secretary. To put it mildly, I found him insulting, crabby, rude, and, at times, obnoxious. I later found out he had a hard time keeping a secretary. More than once, I cried because of his short temper. Both Marie and Mom encouraged me to quit.

"You don't need this." Marie said. "There are other jobs out there."

I agreed, but I had also met plenty of outstanding people there

116

whose company I found delightful. The company had bowling teams, golf tournaments, and weekly meetings in the downstairs bar just for camaraderie. I loved it, and wasn't about to give it all up because of a cranky boss. I learned to deal with Mr. Stubblefield, making sure he found his office clean and dusted in the morning, with all the necessary files on his desk. I had Donna, Mr. Strong's secretary, check over my letters, which Mr. Stubblefield dictated to me the day before. This eliminated errors or helped me interpret his dictation accurately. It took time, but finally worked.

Actually, events worked in my favor, because that same year, the department next to ours needed a secretary. They had solicited my help many times when they were overloaded with work. Mr. Beals, the head of the department, had six men working under him. I became good friends with all of them when I typed their forms and large statistical tabulations. They knew I wasn't happy with Mr. Stubblefield and suggested I apply for the position. After interviewing others, Mr. Beals offered me the job and I happily accepted. The day I cleared my desk to move to my new department, Mr. Stubblefield asked me to think it over and stay. It wasn't easy to look at a white-haired old man as tears filled his eyes, but nothing could keep me from moving on. I gathered up my belongings and left.

I delighted in my new situation, where I felt free to think and contribute. Let's see, there was Chic, Bob, Jim, Gene, Al and George, and of course, Mr. Beals, the boss. I found him charming, gracious, and all the things Mr. Stubblefield wasn't. They were all engineers and a new dawn arose for me each morning as I flew out of bed to dress for work.

The family noticed the change. I had places to go and things to do even on weekends, as fellow employees called to invite me to dinners, theater, and parties.

I overhead Daddy in the parlor one evening say to Mom, "She's never home." He missed his card partner. I can't count the Saturday evenings I spent playing pinochle with him and Mom. As much as I loved him, I felt glad to give it up.

Before I left Mr. Stubblefield's department, a curious thing happened. My desk faced the Drafting Department. As I typed, I could look down the lane to all the drafting tables and the men who sketched and developed meter stations, compressor stations, and the underground pipelines that brought gas flowing into homes across the nation. Another single employee, Donna, and I often walked through the Drafting Department with an ulterior motive. Donna's sway as she walked caused heads to turn and faces to smile.

One day, a drafting table that had stood empty for quite a long time suddenly had an occupant. He was slender, handsome, and shy. His smile revealed the most perfect set of white teeth I had ever seen. Bud was Italian and his dark, smooth-textured skin made his teeth look even brighter. The head of the department, Al, insisted I meet him. Probably because my four-foot, eleven-inch body needed someone no more than five feet eight inches, and Bud fit those measurements.

In spite of the lesser measurements, Bud was a Texan. Born in Del Valle, he grew up in Austin, Texas, the oldest boy in a family of six children. We saw him all week and, at times, the rest of us congregated down in the bar on Fridays after work. But not Bud. He left on weekends, driving straight through back to Texas to see his family and friends. However, come Monday morning, he'd be back at his drafting table looking healthier, handsomer and browner than the week before.

I found Bud cute, but at the time I was having too much fun to zero in on one person. He joined in on all the single action when he was around. The bowling teams attracted everybody. Everyone took part in the yearly golf tournaments, whether we were good golfers or not, and we all lived for our social gatherings on Friday nights.

As I entered my new experience with loving, sociable people, I bowed to the possibility that a new Italian friend might become more than a friend.

Chapter 19

Marie and Jack's second boy, John George Kedzie, was born December 13, 1954. Mom and Dad finally resigned themselves to having grandchildren around them at all times, so they arranged and rearranged the house for new additions. I stayed put in the upper bedroom on the north side of the house, while the children occupied a smaller room off the master bedroom facing the street. Fortunately, the house was ideally arranged for a large family. Mom and Dad kept the corner bedroom.

In those days, it wasn't unusual for me to wake up on a sunny morning in late May or early June, when clear blue skies looked for entertainment, and announce to Mom in the kitchen that I wanted to paint my room a different color.

"There's nothing wrong with your room," she'd say.

However, my mind was made up and as long as I paid for the paint, hauled the ladder up a long flight of stairs, and did the work, she and Marie didn't object. Jack would walk in after I finished and say, "You're hired."

We all noticed around this time that Daddy wasn't feeling too well. He had a lot of pain in his groin area and Mom decided his complaining had gone on long enough.

"Tomorrow we see a doctor," was all she said.

Again, she pursued Dr. Bergan and he recommended a Dr. Walner at Presbyterian-St. Luke's Hospital. Dr. Walner diagnosed Daddy with a good-size hernia after a thorough examination and x-rays, and scheduled surgery for the following week. We all worried and agonized. After all, Daddy was close to seventy years old and this really sounded like a serious operation. I guess we didn't anticipate Dr. Walner's competency—Daddy came through with flying colors.

Not more than a year or two later, Dr. Walner came through again when Mom's voice felt constantly throaty and guttural. She often lost her voice in the middle of a conversation, resulting in a dry hoarseness. The Christmas holidays that year found her tired and listless. She got through somehow bending over to wrap packages and cook meals, but early January found her in Dr. Walner's office.

"Let's see here, Mrs. Zimardo," he said. "Open wide." That's all it took for him to discover a squiggly growth in the back of her throat.

He scheduled surgery immediately. "You're a lucky, Lady," commented the good doctor. "It's benign."

Through all the births, christenings, and surgeries, I continued dating a couple of guys from work off and on, seeing old friends, and playing pinochle with Mom and Dad on unoccupied Saturday nights. My cute Italian friend, Bud, left the office drafting department and returned to field construction as a surveyor in areas where new pipeline was being installed. Weeks often went by before he came back to the Chicago office. But he'd call each time and we'd arrange to meet others for an evening of fun and entertainment. He moved in with various buddies who also worked for the company. They, in turn, were beginning to match up with other single girls in the company. Twenty-four years old found me still single, living with my parents, and cradling Marie and Jack's second child in my arms as the priest poured water over his head, saying "I baptize thee John George Kedzie in the name of the Father, Son and Holy Ghost."

Chapter 20

Love entered at last when Bud began to call more often and his meter station tours ended. He moved from Downers Grove, Illinois, to Ardmore Avenue in Chicago, and then finally to Deming Place in the downtown area of Chicago. We gathered around our downtown friends, Ken and Esther, and enjoyed tree-trimming parties, potluck dinners, and any-excuse-to-get-together parties just for the hell of it. If you paid attention as the evenings wore on, you noticed how different couples wandered off to be alone. Six couples from the company became man and wife, all within a two-year period. We were one of the couples.

But I'll not get ahead of myself. On November 21, 1955, Florence and Frank brought forth their first son and named him Bruce. By then, Cheryl was five years old and Jamie was three. The older kids, Tommy and Philip, were in school. Marie kicked around the idea of going back to work again, but Grandma Zimardo discouraged that in a hurry. Johnny was still a handful, not to mention all the laundry, cooking, sewing and sundry other things that needed doing. Just watching him knock over the dining room chairs every day as a source of entertainment was enough to discourage anyone.

Mom wasn't up to doing all those chores. She willingly cooked, cleaned up the kitchen three times a day, and never balked about ironing, but when it came to running stairs to the basement for laundry or cleaning house, it was just more than she could handle. A lot of anger came from her tiredness now. If she had the whole house and a child to control, she couldn't deal with it all. Marie resigned herself to staying home, which allowed Mom to devote herself more to Daddy. This enabled a year to go by peacefully, often finding Jack and his two boys clowning on the parlor floor as Grandma yelled to all to settle down.

In spite of the dried grass and patches of snow that surrounded our homes as we searched our skies for a bit of sunshine, our hearts swelled with love over the birth of another child in our family.

While Bruce nursed at his mother's breast and grew in love and strength, an unexpected warm, balmy day slipped in between the icy cold of February and the spring of 1956. Mom and Daddy sat out on the wrought-iron porch bench enjoying the relative warmth. As she draped her heavily sweatered arm around Daddy's shoulder, Mom talked into his ear so he could hear her secrets and plans.

Her sixth sense told her of remarkable things developing between Bud and me, and she passed this information into Daddy's good ear. But she didn't know when, and that created the element of surprise.

It was February 15th. As the aroma of a succulent pork roast wafted from the kitchen oven, Frankie pulled up in front of the house and everyone went into the kitchen for an afternoon cup of coffee and cookies. Frank's head reeled with the delicious smells that came from the kitchen, but the excitement of his newborn son still prevailed as he showed pictures to all around. Just then, Bud and I walked in. After warm greetings, Frank noticed my ring. "What's that on your finger, Babe?" I smiled sheepishly and put my head down as I displayed my beautiful diamond. Bud and I got engaged the evening before on February 14th, Valentine's Day, after bowling. Everyone shared our excitement and I think I heard a sigh of relief as Mom hugged me.

I wanted a September wedding, and Bud agreed. I also wanted

a church service with white gown and veil and a full reception. Nothing elaborate, just nice. But even "just nice" was expensive for most parents during those times—it certainly was for mine. So, Bud and I combined our resources and rented the Buffet Room of Klas's Restaurant on Cermack Road, located on Chicago's west side. They served a complete buffet of German cuisine with music and bar. It was a lovely wedding, our guests agreed.

As my arm slipped into Daddy's to walk down the long aisle in Precious Blood Church, peace overcame anxiety as I reminded myself with a calm certainty that I had selected someone strong, considerate and dependable to share my life.

With Bud's help, we got it all done, even participating in a June wedding planned for our friends, Warren and Pat. We stood up for their wedding and in turn, asked them to take part in ours. Marie and Jack served as matron of honor and best man.

Finding an apartment turned out to be quite an undertaking. After several failed attempts at hunting, we got a call from Jack's sister, Marie, who owned a complex on Lowell Avenue and Irving Park Road.

"Go over and take a look at it," she said. "There's a vacant third-floor apartment. Let me know what you think. Call Frank first so he knows you're coming." Frank was her husband.

Finally, we saw a building more to our expectations. No cobwebs or cracked walls, no doorbells hanging out of their sockets, and the immaculate foyer smelled clean. We were impressed.

Finding a sign that said, "Landlord," Bud and I pushed the doorbell. We sensed that Frank expected us.

"I'll get my keys," he said. "The apartment is on the third floor. Is that a problem?" Frank was a considerate, sweet man I'd met only a couple of times, and Bud didn't know him at all. His thick German accent made him even more loveable as he smiled easily while jangling keys. He led us through a courtyard containing lots of bushes and greenery and we assured him, reluctantly, that a third-floor apartment would be fine. By the time we got to the top, we were huffing and puffing, but seeing this perfect little apartment made the long haul worthwhile.

We saw a kitchen, breakfast area, and large bedroom on the left of the entrance. On the right was a small hall with a bathroom. The hall extended into the living room. The back door off the kitchen opened to a small porch that looked airy and inviting. Down below we saw a passageway wide enough to park a car, and Frank said we could use the washer and dryer in the basement.

We returned to the inside of the apartment, walked through the small kitchen, and examined the large bedroom with closet off the dinette. We admired the large walk-in closet off the living room and I brightened as I saw the window, little suspecting that one day in the not-too-distant future, it would be a baby room.

"It's yours, if you want it," said Frank. "The rent is ninety-six dollars a month, but I'll need a deposit." Bud and I didn't hesitate. Bud wrote him a check and asked if he could move in by the end of the month.

To this day, I remember the appetizing aroma in the foyer on my many trips to our apartment before our wedding. As I opened the entrance door and walked up three flights of stairs, my head swam in the whiffs of pot roast, spaghetti sauce, butter beans, or whatever happened to be on Bud's menu for the day. I knew he loved to work in the kitchen, starting back in his student days. He attended school at University of Texas while working in his cousin Victor's restaurant. But I didn't know the depth of his love for the task. He became our cook and to this day still is.

September 8, 1956, Mr. and Mrs. Buddy Nardecchia

By the time of our September 8th wedding, my sister Marie was pregnant again. While we worked at furnishing the apartment, Marie suffered through another bad pregnancy. She felt nauseated most of the time and slept often. In addition to her physical misery, an issue surfaced that had stayed dormant for some time, in spite of considerable conversation that went around and around about it. Marie and Jack wanted to move into a house of their own.

Jack's sister worked in real estate. She was darn good at what she did and when she saw a good buy, she'd spread it around to friends and relatives. She invited Marie and Jack over one evening to talk about this one house on Kostner, right off Irving Park Road. "It needs work, but it's a damn good buy," she said. They toured the house and both of them saw its potential, even though Jack would have to spend a lot of time in remodeling. The building contained two flats, which sparked their interest. They liked the idea that they could rent out the second-floor seven-room apartment. To no one's surprise, Mom objected.

"You and Daddy come with us. Come see for yourselves the possibilities in this house," Marie coaxed. Mom found numerous reasons why they couldn't move at this particular time: "You're pregnant, you're sick, you've got two children that need your full-time protection." She went on and on with little or no encouragement. The truth of the matter was, she just didn't want to move. But she lost when Jack settled the argument. "You either come with us or find some place else to live, because we are putting this house up for sale." This didn't sit well with Mom and Dad because they had helped Marie and Jack financially many times over the years.

I can't tell you how many times Mom called Jack a son-of-a-bitch after that.

126

Chapter 21

Natural Gas Pipeline Company of America changed its name to Mid-Con Corporation and moved to Michigan Avenue. Bud and I hopped the Northwestern train every morning and returned every evening with plans for furnishing our apartment. We spent a good deal of time painting and freshening the place. I ordered a pecan bedroom set that caught my eye in one of the many magazines I thumbed through daily, and Marshall Field's delivered it. We picked up numerous items here and there and we began to grow in our new world. And growth came in other ways.

Six months into our new marriage, my eyes began to droop at the typewriter, and lunch didn't settle right; a sort of nausea crept up and little things irritated me. June brought on a couple of unbearable hot days and all in all, I felt miserable. A trip to the doctor solved the problem when he confirmed I was pregnant. The news staggered both of us.

I was due in December and Marie had Bobby in May. The pregnancy exhausted her. She spent the whole nine months nauseated, tired, and tense. Mom and Jack quarreled often over incidental small things that escalated with time. Mostly, the arguments were over the move into the house on Kostner Avenue. Mom kept saying, "This is not the time" and Jack always answered, "There may not be another time."

Of course, his sister Marie was not Mom's favorite person

either because of her role in orchestrating the move in the first place. But after considerable anxiety, the sale on one house finally went through and the purchase price of the Kostner house was met, with everyone helping out in some form or another.

Without any doubt, the house was a good buy—Mom had to admit that herself after the dust settled from the move. The seven-room second floor apartment rented easily. Marie and Jack's first-floor apartment was a jewel with handsome mahogany woodwork cascading through living room, dining room, bedrooms, and bath. The kitchen had yellow walls, new white cabinets, and tile counters. After they added furnishings and special effects, they had themselves a beautiful, loving home with a bay window. The added five hundred dollars a month for the second-floor apartment didn't hurt, either.

Robert John Kedzie, Marie and Jack's third boy, was born May 2, 1957, and no one could figure out what happened to the series of fat, curly-headed, pink-cheeked little boys that she usually bore. Bob was long, skinny and squiggly-marked, with slanted eyes and straight, mousy brown hair. The one thing he had in common with his brothers was his love of food and his constant hunger. Again, the cries of a starving baby rang through the night while his grandmother and father raced around trying to find some substance to shut him up. Baby cereal with formula helped to sustain him to a point, but everything poor little Bobby ate went right through him. It took many months of formula changes, doctor calls, and frustrations before Bob settled down into a reasonable pattern. I say "reasonable" because he still wasn't totally content, just better than before.

While we heaved a sign of relief with Bobby, I got more attention with my due date drawing near. I didn't have pregnancies like Marie, fortunately. After three months I felt wonderful, using up practically all my energy on preparing a nursery. I worked at the office until June of 1957, and willingly gave up my secretarial job to be a mom.

128

First, I hunted down a cradle. I found one at a garage sale that was in excellent condition. Not knowing whether we expected a boy or girl, I skirted the bottom with many yards of yellow polished cotton and white chiffon. I saw a remodeled sewing machine in a thrift store for sixty-eight dollars and bought it. "Why don't you get a brand-new one?" Bud asked.

"No," I answered. "I want to learn on this one first and then one day, I'll buy a new one. " I loved that machine so much, I never did buy a new one. It was an easy-to-use 1935 Singer that never failed.

While Bud cooked, I sewed and knitted baby clothes, blankets, booties, hats, and sweaters. sticking to whites, yellows, and mint green—pinks and blues could come later, I decided. I had all sorts of colors after Mom and Marie hosted a surprise shower. Back then, the sex of a new baby was always a surprise—the ultrasound technology that determines the sex of today's babies came along much later.

We painted the walk-in closet off the parlor, selecting a mint green shade, and furthered the décor with a white baby crib and dresser. We were all set. The bassinette stood in its proper place with diapers and receiving blankets piled high. But the birth wasn't easy and the labor was long. After 25 hours of mini-contractions that never turned into full-blown labor pains, the doctor suggested a Caesarian section.

"She's not dilating beyond a certain millimeter, Mr. Nardecchia," Dr. Klein said. "We need your permission to do a C-section."

Of course, Bud would agree to anything at this point. He wanted his wife and baby back.

Much later, I opened my eyes. Lying flat on my back, I saw the rosary beads hanging over my head. I felt the sharp pain of an incision, but the rosary beads caught my attention. The hand that held them trembled slightly and my eyes began to focus around the room until they landed on this troubled man praying. He felt relieved and rewarded when he saw my eyes open. God was good.

"It's a sweet little girl, Helen," Bud said, smiling from ear to ear.

I mentally reviewed a list of possible girls' names that ran through my mind, forgetting that we had settled on Karen Marie. Drugs play games with your mind. As tears filled my eyes, I remember saying only one thing.

"How much did she weigh?" Why this mattered so much, I don't know.

"Five pounds, thirteen ounces," he said.

"Wow," I thought as my mind wavered in and out. "She made it!" No incubator as the doctor feared. With Christmas just two weeks away, we had the best gift possible: a beautiful little girl.

03   03   03

Daddy turned seventy years old the year Karen and Bobby were born. His health began to fail a few years earlier, and we all agreed that he needed to take it easy. His memory was worse than his health. Each day after Karen's afternoon nap, I bundled her up and walked down three flights of stairs to the buggy I left parked in the foyer. Every day except for weekends, I walked the long block to Kostner Avenue from Lowell, where we lived, to visit Mom, Dad, and Marie. Bobby and Karen kicked and cooed together in the playpen while I chatted with Mom and Marie. Daddy's hearing wasn't any better, if not worse, and he silently watched the kids in the playpen.

We worried about Daddy, especially after Mom gave us some clues about the situation.

"He doesn't know who you are after you and Karen leave," she said one day. "He sleeps practically all day and can't remember anything."

Everyone realized the seriousness of this failure a few weeks later, after Mom had a long conversation with Frankie about Dad's condition. They discussed his behavior over a hot cup of coffee whenever Frank dropped by the neighborhood.

On the same warm summer day, while noises and breezes flowed through our opened back door, the phone rang right after lunch. I had just put Karen down for a nap.

"Helen, is Daddy over there?" Marie asked.

"No," I answered. "Why, what's wrong?"

"He's gone. We can't find him. We've looked all over—in the basement, upstairs. He's not here." Marie sounded frantic and I could barely imagine what Mom must be going through.

As much as I hated to wake Karen, I had to. She and I hiked our long haul down the stairs and speedily walked over to Kostner Avenue. I could feel the tension when I walked through the door. Mom sat in a living room chair, her hand on her forehead. She looked up as I came through the door with Karen in my arms.

"Oh, Helen, she moaned. "I'm so worried about him."

"He's okay, Mom." Tears welled in my eyes. "Don't worry. God will take care of him."

Frank was there. "Hi Babe," he said. He tried to stay cool and worked at keeping panic down, but his eyes showed deep concern and his hands trembled as he lit a cigarette. Jack came home from work after Marie called him. As he took Karen in his arms and cuddled her, she smiled for him.

We had to conclude that Daddy just walked out of the house, but could not determine where he went. I called Bud.

"I'll come home," he said.

Marie called the police, and neighbors congregated in front of our house offering to help in any way they could.

Family and friends scoured the neighborhood looking for him, with no results. Some of us didn't know what to do with ourselves through the long, worrisome, even tearful wait. We could only think of our dear Daddy roaming around somewhere out there in complete bewilderment, not knowing anyone or where to go. The whole family was frantic. Mary, Joe, and Florence called constantly while we all waited anxiously, minds filled with devastating thoughts. Would someone hurt him? Perhaps knock him down and steal his wallet, or even kill him? We prayed—oh, how we prayed.

Finally, the phone rang at midnight. Frank stayed there overnight, but Bud, Karen, and I returned home with the promise that Marie and I keep in touch. The phone rang twice and Marie grabbed the receiver.

"Mae, this is Johnny Kozie. I don't know if you remember me, but I knew your brother, Frank. We lived near you on Claremont Street. I'm an officer at Precinct 34 and I recognized your father at once. We picked him up roaming Taylor Street. He was terribly confused and lost."

Marie turned to Frankie. "They've found him. This is a police officer and he knows you." Frankie grabbed the phone.

"Yeah, hello," he said.

"Johnny! Yeah."

"We've been so worried. He's okay, eh?"

"We'll be right there."

"Come on, Jack. He's at a police station on Taylor Street. He was trying to go back to the old neighborhood." They hurried out the door as Mom broke down with tears of relief.

We viewed Daddy's return as something to celebrate, even though Mom saw signs of terror in his eyes and his wallet was gone. Frank and Jack found him with a bruise on his forehead and we surmised that either he fell, or someone hit him. Marie told us about his dirty shirt and torn pants when she called at two o'clock in the morning, but he was home and that's all that mattered.

Daddy was never the same again, however. Sadly, his mind had deteriorated so badly that he hardly remembered our mother. More than once he ordered her out of his bed, claiming he was a married man and didn't fool around with other women. Sad-but also comical at times.

We kept a watchful eye on Daddy. Mom always sat with him

on the front porch, but he showed no further desire to wander and settled down into a comfortable routine. Even though his hearing never improved, he managed to participate in some way during parties and yearly gatherings. When Mom suggested two-hand rummy, he couldn't remember all of the game, and that got worse with time. Mainly, he roamed in our midst, smiling occasionally and sleeping often.

Chapter 22

During the time Bud and I worked, I never used the basement appliances. I took our clothes to a Laundromat instead. But after Karen's birth and as she got older, I began to use the facilities on weekends while Bud babysat.

I always dragged a laundry bag down the stairs early Saturday morning, sorted clothes, and started a load. With a steady routine upstairs, sometimes I wouldn't get back down to the basement until late in the evening. The darkness frightened me and my imagination ran wild as I hurried through each load. Dragging baskets of clothes up three flights of stairs grew increasingly wearisome and Bud realized the wear and tear of it all.

Our neighbor across the hall, Mary Hausher, gladly took Karen on Sundays while we attended Mass at St. Edward's Parish, but asking her to mind Karen while I did laundry seemed too much of an imposition and I just didn't want to do that.

One afternoon after returning from visiting Mom, Marie, and Daddy, I decided to meander around our building pushing Karen in the stroller. She wore her pink bonnet and lightweight jacket while a warm blanket covered her legs and protected her from the cool breezes of May. As I zipped up my wrap, I saw our landlord, Frank, thinning bushes at the front of the building.

He hailed me down. "Say," he said. "The apartment here on the first floor is going to be vacant and I wonder if you'd like to have it. We see you hauling your bags of laundry from the third floor. This would be better for you."

My excitement grew as I thought about it, and that evening I passed it on to Bud.

"Let's consider it," he said. Karen was four months old and we had just discovered that I was pregnant again. To rid my life of three flights of stairs carrying groceries, laundry, and a child seemed like the answer to a prayer. Four months into my pregnancy we made the move down, but we didn't lose our across-the-hall friend.

Mary Hausher was in her late fifties or early sixties, and had never married. She absolutely loved Karen. Quite often she delighted Karen with little gifts, and Christmas always brought a new storybook that ranged from *The World of Pooh* to the Dr. Seuss collection.

Mary also loved Bud's cooking, particularly his fabulous salad dressings that he prepared himself, and we often sought each other out on a Saturday night for cocktails, steak dinners, and vinaigrette salads as the smell of fresh garlic, sweet basil, and oregano permeated our five-room apartment.

Mary loved horse racing. Once a year on a warm June or July day, her brother picked her up and off to the races they went. Then he passed away. Since we lived no more than a thirty-mile drive from Arlington Park, we offered to take Mary to the races as a birthday treat. The smile that crossed her face told us we had picked the right gift.

That's all it took for us to become racing fans as well. Marie took Karen to play with Bobby while the three of us spent an afternoon in the sun betting on the gray horse or a well-known jockey. Mary and I were jockey betters, but Bud often disappeared to look over the condition of the horse. He'd return and we'd all quietly place our bets. We never won big, but we won a deep friendship with Mary that lasted for a good many years.

And to her delight, another little girl, who we named Kathryn

Lynn, was born January 12, 1959. Dr. Klein wasn't taking any chances on long labor again, so he once again recommended a Caesarian section.

"Because of those little babies you have, Helen," he commented on one of my monthly visits, "I'm suggesting that we keep the baby in the womb up to as close to your due date as possible. Please don't go into labor and get me out of bed one o'clock in the morning."

Strangely, that's exactly what happened. Kathy weighed in at five pounds six ounces and they immediately placed her in an incubator. "Another little girl," Dr. Klein told Bud right after the delivery. "A minute later and the baby would have been too far into the birth canal to perform Caesarian. Now, I'm going home to get some sleep."

I came to in a large ward filled with women. All had natural births and I watched them walk around, laughing and talking, as I laid in severe pain with a reopened incision from my navel all the way down. When a pretty blonde nurse checked my blood pressure, I stared at her blue eyes and red lipstick and remember saying, "Is the baby okay?"

"Oh, she's a darling, would you like to see her?"

I said, "No." As I think back, that was an awful thing to say. I should have said, "Not yet."

At the same time, Bud came in. He had been tied up in the hall talking to an intern after a long view of Kathy.

"Hey," he said. "How you feeling?" He carried an armful of beautiful roses, which the blonde nurse took away after adjusting her blue sweater around her shoulders. A few minutes later she placed them at the side of my bed in a vase of water.

"I feel terrible. Lots of pain this time, Bud," was my answer. I remember my pediatrician, glasses hanging on the tip of his nose, asking if I would nurse the baby. Lying flat on my back because it hurt so much to turn, I remarked, "Dr. Klein preferred I didn't."

Dr. Harrison, tugging at his tie and acting like his usual feisty self, returned, "What do you think you have those two things for?"

I choose to ignore him and instead asked to see Kathy, realizing I needed to perk up. Her vital signs were so good that she only stayed a short time in the incubator. When they placed Kathy on my stomach, I felt much happier. I smiled at Bud as she sucked her fist. She raised her uncontrollable eyes and wiggled. As she snuggled close to my breasts, I remember thinking this one would be beautiful. And she was.

My stay ended after eight long days in a chaotic hospital that was undergoing remodeling and expanding. From the large ward, I transferred to a two-bed room with a shortage of nurses, and all the ones I met had short tempers. I will never forget one in particular who snapped back no matter what I asked because she felt so overworked and tired. I celebrated the day Bud wheeled me to our car to go home. The sight of a jubilant Karen and smiling Aunt Marie in the back seat erased all of my pain and misery. After settling into the seat with our adorable little baby girl on my lap, a smile crossed my lips as Bud asked his favorite question, "What do you want for dinner?"

"Make it for two more," Marie said laughing cheerfully.

"Oh, will you and Jack join us?" I asked.

"No," she said. "I'm eating for two again."

My head swung around and we laughed.

"Does Mom know?" I asked.

"The baby's due in October," she said with a huge smile. "I'll wait a while to tell her."

Chapter 23

I didn't want to break the news. Bud and I had been looking in different areas at homes for sale. The down payments required seemed out of our reach, but we had to do something to remedy the congestion and crowded living arrangement we had. Washing clothes in a dark, damp basement and trekking up stairs grew increasingly wearisome. First floor or third floor, it didn't matter. The inconvenience for four people wore me out.

As soon as Kathy outgrew the yellow organdy cradle, we would have to jam a full-size crib in a corner with little or no walking space. We felt we had no choice. But I delayed telling Mom and Marie about our plans to move. They wanted us to always stay nearby, I knew.

While we continued to research and follow up on ads, we invited Mom and Dad over on a particular Sunday afternoon for dinner. Thinking back on this occasion, I remember being surprised that Mom agreed to come.

"I'll have Bud come over to get you," I said.

"No," she answered. "A walk would be good for us."

It was a warm summer day and I considered her suggestion sensible.

They walked over. The day was divine. Bud cooked a delicious spaghetti dinner. Daddy raved about his sauce and Grandma Zimardo enjoyed the two little grandchildren.

"I think we should leave before it gets dark," Mom remarked after a couple of hours. She began searching the parlor for her purse.

Bud was all set to drive them home, but again, Mom said, "No, the walk will do us good."

We walked them down the first floor flight of steps, holding the children in our arms. Mom grabbed Daddy's arm and they strolled off.

We didn't worry. In fact, we never gave it another thought until the phone rang an hour later. Then I heard my sister Marie chewing me up and down and berating me right and left for allowing them to walk home.

It seems Mom stepped off the curb to cross the street as the light turned green at Kostner and Irving Park Road. They were no more than a half block away from home, in broad daylight. Although Mom kept holding Daddy's arm, her foot twisted and she went down. A large gentleman standing nearby, saw it happen. He helped her up and escorted them both home.

Marie was frantic and she did not waste words on me. My knees buckled and I immediately left the kids in Bud's care to see how badly Mom had been hurt. At this time in her life, she was a big woman weighing every bit of one hundred and eighty pounds, so her fall had to be serious.

I found her bruised around the head and the side of her face. She seemed terrified and said she hurt all over. Daddy was totally confused, and not quite sure what happened. No words could explain my guilt, my culpability, my bitter regret for letting them walk home alone, so I said nothing to Marie. I knew her anxiety. These two people were her responsibility, and I let her down.

The aftermath of this fall could be a book in itself.

In their move from Claremont Street, Mom and Dad lost Dr. Bergan and started seeing a neighborhood doctor on Irving Park Road. I couldn't even tell you his name now—I don't remember it. They went to him for minor complaints. During this dialog, we will call him Dr. Malito. I know he was Italian.

Marie called Dr. Malito and he actually made a house call. After checking Mom's vital signs, he said, "She's just bruised badly, but she'll be all right." He suggested no X-rays, no further checking of any kind.

But clearly, Mom wasn't all right. She suffered episodes of confusion, vision problems, and headaches. She got stronger eyeglasses and she took medications to calm her, but her headaches persisted. Finally, after months of medical problems and another tumble down the back porch stairs because of disorientation, a huge lump showed itself on her right hip. She was literally bent in half and could barely walk as this monstrous growth grew bigger on her body.

Dr. Malito said it was a cyst, and we should be prepared because one day it would burst. He told Marie to keep large towels handy at all times. In the meantime, Mom began to lose sleep and experienced tremendous stress.

Finally, after pressure from all the adult members of the family, Marie called Dr. Walner, the physician who performed the operation on Mom's throat and Daddy's hernia.

"Bring her to the emergency room tomorrow morning," he said. "I'll take a look at her."

I packed early in the morning and walked over to watch Bobby, Karen, and Kathy so Marie and Jack could take Mom to Presbyterian-St. Luke's Emergency Ward. They hospitalized her immediately and made arrangements to drain the giant-sized cyst that grew out of her hip.

Dr. Walner said, "That cyst was crippling her, and poison could have eventually invaded her blood stream." He said it would never have burst on the outside. Had we pursued the issue, Dr. Malito could have had a lawsuit on his hands. In today's world, he would have been sued big-time.

Mom recovered, but not until after further surgery. After extensive tests, the doctors discovered that her right kidney was smashed against the wall of her body and it had to be removed. It took months for Mom to regain her strength and return to some degree of normalcy. We always felt the trauma of this accident took a great toll on her and affected her spirit.

But the peaks and valleys of life produce laughter one day and tears another. While we worried and prayed for Mom to recover, Marie's big stomach, dented and pounded from little feet, began to drop. It was the first week of October 1960, and time was running out.

We waited anxiously, all joining in the hope for a little girl, but God loved Marie's boys so much that he sent her another one. Michael John Kedzie was born October 12th, 1960, but again, complications ensued. Michael arrived with jaundice, requiring that new blood be pumped into his veins. It was touch and go, but done successfully by skilled doctors.

The parents brought home another cherub-faced infant. Maybe not so pink this time—a little more on the pale side—but plump and pretty with very blond hair and blue eyes.

Grandma's comment when she saw him: "He's a pretty little boy, but I hope you're through this time, Jack Kedzie."

Mom was always an open book. Whatever she thought, she said.

Chapter 24

The eventful year of 1961 began with a mild spring. Though signs of spring arrived with an occasional bud or two, March was notoriously unstable in Chicago. One day could call for a window cracked for warm breezes, and another day the same window slammed shut because of a snowstorm.

On one relatively mild Saturday, Bud suggested we travel to a suburb called Palatine to look at a few model houses.

The ad in the paper assured interested buyers that a veteran's loan could apply to purchases.

Palatine was in the far end of Chicago, about thirty-five miles northwest of where we lived and not far from towns like Arlington Heights, Schaumburg, Hoffman Estates, and Barrington. I shuddered to think about moving so far from family, especially with Daddy's worsening mental condition. But we went to see.

We saw three models, but the one that appealed to us the most was a ranch about 1400 square feet, with three bedrooms and two baths. Bud liked the large kitchen, which had an attached utility room and a door leading out to a one-car garage. The front door opened to a foyer extending to a combination family room/dining area. To the right of the foyer, at the entrance, we saw the bathroom and three bedrooms. The left of the foyer had a parlor. It seemed really perfect for us, but we still felt unsure. We really hadn't looked much anywhere else and felt we should.

As we mused and considered, Daddy's health grew worse.

He began to swell up, bloat, and experience severe pain. When

I visited him, he didn't know who I was and asked Mom each time, "Who was the lady that comes here with her two kids every day? She should stay home and take care of them." Although everyone thought it was funny, my heart broke because he didn't know me anymore.

Then in the month of April, what we most feared happened. I saw Daddy stretched out on his bed completely dressed as I entered the bedroom. Frankie would arrive soon to accompany him to the hospital. Clearly, his condition was serious.

I remember saying, "You're going to be okay, Daddy," as I laid my hand on his bloated stomach. Tears filled my eyes and I kissed his cheek. He smiled and said, "Helen, it's okay, don't worry. I've lived a good life. It's time to go."

It was the first time in years that he made sense and called me by my name. I crumpled.

The ambulance pulled up and took Daddy to the hospital, along with Frank and Marie. The phone rang at midnight and I heard Frankie's voice saying, "Babe, Daddy's gone." After a hernia erupted near his lower bowel, the blood poisoning that seeped through his bloodstream went straight to his heart.

We gathered at St. Viator's Church on Sunnyside Avenue for a Requiem Mass. The grandchildren, with Mary and Joe's son Tommy being the oldest, all realized our loss and felt our pain. Quietly, they surrounded Grandpa's casket as Father Kelly blessed it with incense and prayer. The smell of the burnt ashes escaped throughout the church and we all held our heads down low.

The Ave Maria caused Mom to break down. She shook with sorrow as she sobbed into her handkerchief, and Jack wrapped her in his arms. The funeral saddened us deeply, and why not? We had not experienced death as a family before.

On April 6, 1961, Jasper Zimardo, seventy-five years old, was laid to rest in St. Joseph's cemetery as the mingled smell of spring blossoms and funeral bouquets filled the air.

Chapter 25

Karen was close to four years old and Kathy three when we again pursued the tedious chore of finding a home of our own. We had searched numerous Chicago areas without luck, and decided to once again visit the quaint but thriving town of Palatine. This time we took Jack and Marie along. We wanted their opinion on the ranch we had visited in the past. They approved of our choice. Marie loved the arrangement of the house and we all agreed that a half-hour drive from Chicago wasn't so bad. As Marie told Mom, "At least they're not moving to Texas."

So with no further ado, we selected a lot on Bissell Drive. With our veteran's loan, we only needed a small down payment of approximately three hundred dollars to begin construction, and our excitement grew.

Every weekend, rain or shine, we drove to Palatine with mounting anticipation of our move-in date. When November and December arrived, we bundled up the kids in winter snowsuits and boots to crunch through the packed snow that surrounded our new home to be.

Moving day arrived the following January of 1962 on one of the coldest days of the year, with snow drifts up to twenty inches. On that day Karen ran a temperature of a hundred and one, with Kathy close behind fighting a bad cold.

We had packed for weeks, sadly saying goodbye to Mary

Hauscher and our other friends in the building. We made Mary promise she'd visit us and she did every Christmastime, bringing the girls their desired books: *Little Women, Hans Christian Andersen,* and *Gulliver's Travels,* among others.

The day of departure, Buddy drove to Palatine with movers to heat the house and help erect beds, as I bundled the children and wrapped them in warm blankets. Within a couple of hours we all headed on our way, driving the Kennedy toll roads to Palatine, but my mind focused on only one thought: to find a doctor. Karen's temperature kept rising and she was burning up. Buddy returned again to the apartment in Chicago to direct the moving at that end.

Our telephone had been installed the day before and a directory of Palatine and other towns sat close by. I found a Dr. O'Connor nearby and called the number.

She sounded gracious, but not very willing to come out in the terrible blizzard that was building until I told her about our circumstances. I didn't drive and had no car even if I did, and Karen's virus had grown to a full-blown flu with vomiting and diarrhea. I had even searched the block for a neighbor, but only one house on the block had an occupant and she wasn't home. When the doctor's car pulled into our driveway, I thanked the Blessed Mother with my entire heart and soul.

Dr. O'Connor's examination confirmed it was a bad virus and prescribed an antibiotic. She gave me the name of the pharmacy in a strip mall not too far from home, and dropped the prescription off on the way back to her office. The store delivered, and Karen had to take the medication for ten days. Dr. O'Connor also allowed for a refill in case Kathy followed up with the same symptoms. Surely, God does send angels when the going gets tough.

The kids got better and a normal life evolved as more houses went up on Bissell Drive and people moved in. We returned often to visit Mom and the Kedzies, and we all took turns at holiday time for family reunions.

Joe and Frank still conducted their usual playful arguments

that always ended with, "You don't know what the hell you're talking about." Only now, Bud got interested and jumped in whenever they'd let him. Both Joe and Frank viewed him as a fellow Marine buddy from Texas, but not in controversial subjects. As Frank remarked, "Watch that Buddy. He's a fooler."

Mom loved our house, but as she got older she never strayed too often from Jack and Marie, always informing us that Marie needed her.

And Marie probably did to a point, with four rambunctious boys, but a break from Mom's incessant nagging might have helped. Jack and Marie just couldn't do anything right in Mom's eyes, and she let everyone know it. After a while, friends and relatives ignored her remarks and mostly enjoyed her company on the sunny front porch comfortably arranged with cushioned chairs.

We also added cushioned benches and chairs to our backyard furniture after we met an affable neighbor down the street. He stood close to seven feet tall, lanky and handsome in his own way. Actually, we met Mike through our children when he walked Karen home. The sight of him frightened me at first when I opened the front door, but I saw smiles and relaxed as Kathy came running behind laughing. Little three-foot-tall Karen held Mike's finger.

"She said I should meet you," chirped Mike.

The girls had been playing out front with friends, and Karen left the others to sit on the curb and talk to Mike as he weeded.

"She's amazing," Mike said. "Talking to her is like talking to an adult."

With that, he extended his hand and said, "I'm Mike Yack. Eileen and I live in the house on the corner."

Eileen and Mike had only been married about three years when we met. It was a second marriage for Eileen and her son, Kip, was a darling-fourteen-year old who became our babysitter. The girls loved his puppet performances that he improvised with ease.

Many times they'd ask me, "Mom are you going out tonight

146

so Kip can come over?"

But the friendship really developed over chicken livers. Chicken livers? Yes. Bud and Mike both cooked out often and in any kind of weather. While Mike often smelled our steaks cooking on Saturday night, one day Buddy picked up an aroma coming from Mike's house, that whetted his appetite with a strong desire. Finally, he couldn't stand it any longer. He walked across the backyards and asked simply, "What are you cooking?"

In a square pan lying on the coals he saw a pan of chicken livers gloriously surrounded with Chicago Style Hot Giardiniera peppers soaking in virgin olive oil. A pungent aroma rose from the pan. After that we became good friends and met many Saturdays at cocktail time to sip martinis while chicken livers and peppers soaked in olive oil.

Through all of this I became pregnant again, for our longing to have a little boy never left us. "Let's try one more time," we decided.

I loved Christmas more than any other time of year. After doling out way too many gifts to the girls and singing loudly around the piano at the Yacks' house as Eileen played, my symptoms of pregnancy began. I wasn't aware that it was pregnancy at first. I thought it may just be a flu thing, but continuous nausea and a trip to Dr. Klein confirmed the truth.

After the delivery, our child's weight created such excitement for Dr. Klein that he forgot to mention the sex.

Dressed in operating attire and cap, he swung into the waiting room looking for Bud.

"There you are," he said. "Boy, have I got good news for you. The baby weighed six pounds, three ounces. The best yet!"

It took Bud a while to settle him down. Finally he asked, "What was it, a boy or girl?"

"Oh, it was a boy," the good doctor said, and Bud practically bounced off the ceiling with exhilaration.

He became David: David Joseph Nardecchia, born October 2,

1963.

"I knew it was a boy," I exclaimed confidently.

"And how did you know that?" asked Bud.

"The nurse held him up in the nursery as they wheeled me past and I saw his burly big chest. No little girl has a chest like that."

But sadness followed on the heels of David's birth as we watched the assassination of John F. Kennedy, the thirty-fifth president of the United States, on television one month later. The events of November 22, 1963 shocked our nation to a standstill. We spent days, weeks, and months agonizing over each despairing detail of the story. We learned to hate Lee Oswald and Jack Ruby for upsetting our Camelot, then dragging our nation's good name through the mud of insolence, especially since we felt such excitement, along with President Kennedy, about his dream of landing a man on the moon.

As we listened to the story unfold, we began to realize that we were not a nation loved by all around the world. We wondered then, and we still wonder now, if someone across the waters envied his power and arranged the whole thing. Only God knows.

So as I cried with others through the first weeks of this awful crime, things began happening again with family. Marie and Jack's boys were about to have a little brother or sister.

We all noticed that Marie carried this baby differently: not so big and cumbersome this time, but rounder and seemingly more comfortable looking. Maybe there is something to how a mother looks carrying a boy or girl. Who knows?

When her time came upon us, little Mari Lynn was alive but not for long. She expired about five hours after birth with a collapsed lung. It was too sad for words—not just for a week or a month, but for a long, long time. Marie hid herself in her room after the funeral and turned away from life. Daddy's grave was opened and Mari Lynn's tiny casket was placed on top of his. Marie wanted it that way.

Jack worried terribly about her, and Mom's nervousness gave way to words that she never should have said.

"Well, she's just going to have to get over this. Lots of mothers lose babies. I can't handle this big household by myself." We all wanted to smack her.

Consoling Marie and Jack didn't help. Mary, Florence, and I called often but none of this seemed to make matters better. Even Frankie made his weekly trips to the house, but Marie wanted little to do with anyone. Finally Marie, realizing that Jack and the boys needed her, woke up early one morning to fix a large batch of pancakes. No more babies came. Jack and Marie resigned themselves to being content with their four boys.

Chapter 26

The rains came and came. A torrential downpour hit Palatine and adjacent areas early one April morning and continued for days. After placing David in his cradle, I spread the parlor sheers on the window to peek out, watching and worrying about the possibility of a flood. It was Saturday and most cars were tucked in garages, for the streets looked desolate.

I saw our neighbor, Mr. Gordon, come out every so often covered in a hooded slicker to check the storm sewer in front of his house. The water kept building up and not draining. As tree branches and debris collected there, he kept reaching down and clearing the area, hoping the water would go down. It never did.

Finally, as the rain slammed down on the street and pavement, an overflow of water began to soak the lawn and seep down his slanted driveway. With Mrs. Gordon, a terminal cancer patient, held up in an upstairs bedroom, Mr. Gordon worried about a basement family room and bath built below ground level.

It rained all night and the next day, never letting up. People in other houses on the block kept checking their windows to see just how drastic the situation would become. Finally, the worst happened. The storm sewers stop accepting the water and spilled over onto the lawns in huge amounts. The pipes proved too small for the tremendous gush of water, and Mr. Gordon's house suffered the most. A constant flow of water slid down his driveway into the garage and basement family room.

Neighbors covered in slickers and boots waded over to help him. They piled furniture high or carried it upstairs into the kitchen, dining room, or wherever they might hope to protect it. Bud and others pushed themselves through waist-high water in the garage and family room as the waters mounted.

Our prayers were finally answered when the rains began to slow down late that evening, and by morning it had stopped. The newspapers called it a "monsoon," and some of us fared better than others. Mrs. Gordon was taken to her daughter's house as cleanup began in their household. Everyone who could helped. In just a matter of months, Mrs. Gordon passed away and the house went up for sale.

But in the meantime, the city sent out construction workers to jackhammer the streets along the curb to plant larger pipe so that such a catastrophe wouldn't happen again. We had lived in Palatine twenty-five years and never saw the likes of that devastation again. But I do remember how neighbors congregated in our kitchen when a below-zero frost caused the electric power to go off in our homes. We had the only house on the block with gas appliances. Since it was early in the afternoon, I invited all the mothers with children to come over and warm up on folding chairs placed around the oven as the trees, clotheslines, and fences outside our windows dripped with icicles.

ୠ   ୠ   ୠ

A young Italian family with three children bought the Gordon house. Joe worked for United Airlines and Toni was a housewife expecting another child. The neighborhood welcomed them as they joined our block parties and socials. The new baby was a girl.

When I remember Delores and Bob, who lived across the street from us, I think back on the friendship that developed between their daughters and ours. Their daughter Barb and our

Karen displayed great ingenuity in creating plays and stage parts that they performed in our garage. "Music Man" was their favorite. They pantomime the words to all the songs off a 78 rpm record swirling on an old recorder in the corner of the garage. They hung old bedspreads and huge sheets for scenery. The audience enjoyed popcorn and cold pop before, during, and after the show. Delores and I kept the refreshments coming while neighbors and their children sat in folding chairs strewn around the garage.

I remember Anne, Delores' second daughter, dressed in Bob's suit and an old straw hat and waving a baton, starting off the show. "Ladies and gentlemen!" she bellowed. "Sit back and enjoy our rendition of the *Music Man.* Robert Preston would have smiled proudly as he watched our Kathy playing Marian the Librarian, singing "Till There Was You."

Truly, these are what dreams are made of.

After a while, the neighborhood kids grew up, houses sold, and families went their own ways. But while we were there together, we all had delightful fun sharing the camaraderie.

We all loved the excitement of blocking off the street for games, barbecues, corn on the cob, beer, and ice cream, which then developed into music and dancing to all hours.

This didn't happen just one time but every year for many years, always adding new neighbors.

"Hit it, Bob! Get it over the net," Bob's wife Delores shouted enthusiastically, and the volleyball went flying over a long net tied from one tree to another across the length of the street. Everyone joined in, even the kids, leaving only the elders to watch the food. The delightful food aromas and a strenuous game of volleyball always increased the appetite.

The next morning, one by one, all the neighbors dragged out of their houses to start the cleanup, dumping stray beer cans, burnt corn husks, and loose debris into large garbage bags. The big, husky guys carried all the barbecue pits back to their owners, and the sweep crew assembled to clean the street. After a crew took the wooden horses down, the block returned to normal and most of us went back to bed to catch up on sleep.

As new neighbors moved in and out of Palatine, my siblings began to spread apart and move to different parts of Illinois. Joe and Mary bought a home in Westchester and Florence and Frank established their home in River Forest. We stayed in Palatine, while Jack and Marie continued on with Mom on Kostner Avenue. Though we all lived farther apart, we always made a point to gather together at holiday time.

We generally celebrated Thanksgiving at Marie and Jack's house, mainly because Mom, in her late sixties now, felt happier staying home and making her bread dressing. We never learned her secret for making lasagna and bread dressing so delicious. Though we all made the attempt, we never seemed to get it quite right. Actually, Bud's lasagna was voted in second place but he opted for his mother's cornbread turkey dressing which didn't always go over with Chicagoans. But without a doubt, everyone stood in line for Marie's pumpkin or sometimes chiffon pumpkin pies standing alongside the lemon meringue and oozy cinnamon apple.

For some reason, only the women were able to move after dinner. They immediately began cleaning up as Frank, Joe, Jack, and Bud sprawled lifeless across the living room sofa. I'd give anything to have it all back again.

When 1964-65 ushered in, President Lyndon B. Johnson got more involved in the Vietnam War, trying desperately to bring it to an end. The Beatles arrived in America and overwhelmed our nation on the Ed Sullivan Show. Paul McCartney's "Yesterday" and John Lennon's "Imagine" spoke words in song we had never heard before.

But the surprising thing in our family circle was realizing that our oldest boys, Tommy and Philip were already graduating from high school and thinking about college. Philip, an excellent student, had no problems getting into Northwestern. How Jack and

Marie afforded it, I'll never know. Philip's part-time work and living at home did help.

Tommy was also a good student and my brother Joe, was determined he'd go to a first-rate school. Tommy passed the entrance exam and was accepted at Purdue University in Lafayette, Indiana. Philip decided on engineering and Tommy, metallurgy as majors.

Things got better for Marie and Jack as well. They budgeted and lived frugally while Mom aged gracefully, but not always contentedly. She missed Daddy and fell into periods of loneliness, mourning the loss of her mate. She was luckier than most at her age because she had the companionship of a family surrounding her, but we could never make her realize that. She was hard to please.

Chapter 27

As I looked through the window and down several floors of the hospital, I saw my three-year-old son David standing on a wet sidewalk, holding Aunt Marie's hand and looking up. How I longed to hold his sorrowful little face in my hands and kiss his cheek, but the hospital rules didn't allow this.

Once again, I crossed the threshold of Presbyterian-St. Luke's Hospital with Bud after symptoms of pain and irregular vaginal bleeding. A new doctor had entered my life because reliable Dr. Klein passed away.

Dr. Sengson, an Asian doctor, suggested a hysterectomy due to a large cyst that had formed on my left ovary. He also detected several small cysts collecting on the uterus and right ovary. Removal of the uterus and ovaries would correct the irregular bleeding.

Though frightened at first, I discovered by researching Dr. Sengson's medical background that he was a very competent surgeon who had performed this surgery many times. The surgery went well, and as I looked down and waved to David on my sixth day of healing I looked forward to the happiness of arriving home in two more days.

Finally, I heard both doctor and nurse's encouraging words of farewell as they lowered me into a wheelchair. The nurse placed flowers and cards on my lap with a smile. To complete my happiness, all I needed was the sight of Karen, Kathy, and David waving at me from the back seat of the car as I exited the hospital.

"Let's go home," I told Bud as we pulled away from the curb.

Healing came slowly, but it came. After a year of recuperating, I felt my old self again, but I sadly watched as Mom declined. Marie and Jack got her back and forth to the doctors when needed, but doctor reports always said the same thing: "She's getting old."

Mom brightened when her favorite television shows came on but, like all of us, felt very saddened when she heard that Martin Luther King was shot in April of 1968. Her ups and downs came more frequently until it became apparent that she was giving up.

Each year we all gathered together for holidays, but it seemed her energy level sunk lower and her endurance dwindled. When she allowed Marie or Florence to make the lasagna or prepare the Thanksgiving dressing, we knew she was not well.

But we all perked up when nineteen-year-old Philip became engaged to Crystel Stegeman. Phil, fresh out of college, seemed too young to take such an serious step, but they were in love and planned a wedding for March of 1971.

We weren't so sure about Mom attending the wedding, for her health was failing quickly, but she did on the condition that someone would see her home when she had had enough.

But months after the wedding and just short of Christmas, her body finally surrendered. As Bud prepared a birthday dinner for me on December 14th, the phone rang and Frank delivered sad news once again.

"Mom was rushed to the hospital. Her breathing is bad and we'll keep you posted," he said.

Early the next morning we waited and then finally heard that she succumbed. It was December 15, 1971. "She just didn't want to live anymore," said Dr. Walner.

We gathered for her funeral, where tears flowed and children expressed sorrowful faces. Eulogies from the older children

156

brought back happy times with Grandma; Tommy remembering her laughter and Philip the oatmeal cookies with coconut. Philip, tall and handsome in a dark suit, stepped down from the altar and hugged his mother. Tears on his cheek caught the sunlight coming through the high stained glass window.

Our breathing slowed and pain clutched our throats as we watched my sister Marie's trip up the aisle to touch and feel her coffin. Mom's presence, more meaningful to her than any of us because of the care and love given over the many years, caused us to sob as we all gathered around to comfort and be comforted.

With bundled scarves around our faces and heavy coats protecting us from the strong Chicago wind, we cried forlorn tears as we slumped next to one another listening to Father O'Connor's final prayers of departure. The stream of cold air evaporated between us as we listened. Our matriarch was gone.

When I offered to help Marie pack the belongings in our mother's closet some months later, I didn't plan on discovering a flowered, orange and pink hatbox behind an old album she kept for years on her top shelf. We had put off going through her things for months, dreading the tears and heavy heart. I blew at the dust and then reached in the back pocket of my jeans for a cloth. A layer of dust also covered the box and I realized it had been years since anything disturbed the comfortable cobwebs.

Climbing down from the ladder, I sat on the edge of the bed and opened the album. Some familiar faces in the photographs from our past happy years showed Aunt Marie smiling broadly, holding her first grandchild. Another of our brother Joe in his Marine uniform, and a back porch photo of Daddy on Claremont Street brought a warm smile to my lips. Most I had seen before, but looking through them again brought Mom closer, and I could remember her as she once was and not as she looked at the sad hour of her passing. Some pictures slipped from their pasted positions as I set the album aside to reach for the flowered box.

My heart raced as I opened the black two-inch ribbon that tied the lid on the box. There, I found a black and white picture of Joseph T. Dunn, her first husband, a missal yellow with age, and a mother-of-pearl cameo. I smiled at the handsome face of Joe Dunn, and knew instantly why she loved him.

Next, I reached for the cameo, encased in a small gray bag, and held it up to the light to see the delicate detailed work. I saw a mother-of-pearl emblem, embossed higher with a pink background, surrounded with a gold-laced edging. Some of the edging had tarnished, but that made it even more endearing to me.

I folded my legs in front of me and placed the missal snugly on my lap. I noticed it was called a "Manual of Prayer." I opened it slowly, trying to prevent the binding from loosening and breaking away. I assumed it had to be at least seventy-five years old, but then I discovered a prayer pasted on the inside of the cover. On the lead sheet an inscription written by Joe said, "God be with you, from Joseph T. Dunn to Augustine Eiler, December 1st, 1916."

My mind pictured my mother young and beautiful again, with curly fire-red hair arranged under a wide-rimmed hat. She stood next to a tall, slender Joe Dunn wearing a dark suit and white shirt. As I wiped the tears slowly draining down my cheeks, my heart lifted for this lasting picture I would always remember of her. These treasures are mine for a little while. Hopefully, one day one of my daughters will discover an orange and pink hatbox on the shelf of my closet to remind her of those who went before with amazing strength and gentle understanding.

I carried the box into the kitchen to show Marie. With tearful eyes, she touched each item and then carefully handed the cameo to me.

"Here," she said. "Mom would want you to have this.

She had meant to give it to you sooner."

Years later, she gave me the flowered hatbox with The Missal of Prayer and Joe's picture.

Struggling to comprehend Mom's loss over the next couple of years took time. We felt sad that she didn't live long enough to attend her first grandson's wedding. But we all carried her spirit to the chapel at Purdue University as Mr. and Mrs. James Norman and Geneive Mae gave their daughter, Genean Barker, in marriage to Thomas P. Dunn. Soon afterwards, Frank and Florence's daughter, Cheryl, relocated to California in pursuit of other avenues of life and we watched the "flower children" of our era move on to maturity.

The Dunn family

While other families grew, ours did also. During those growing years, we traveled to California for Disneyland and enjoyed business trips to New Orleans and Washington, D.C. Our busy agenda also included a trip with Bud's mother, Sophie, to New Jersey, where she visited her mother and siblings after a long hiatus of not seeing one another. Bud's father, Ben, had died of a heart attack some years earlier.

I remember the sadness of that time, also, and the call that

159

came in while I attended a school meeting. As I crawled into bed after midnight, Bud turned to say his sister called to tell him his Dad passed on after a massive heart attack.

Bud's father had walked to a car dealership in ninety-degree temperatures to buy a part for his car. The day before he witnessed the murder of Texas citizens, gunned down by Charles Whitman as he sprayed bullets from the top of the University of Texas Tower. All this took place in August of 1966.

Bud's mother sobbed as she held her husband's head in her arms after he collapsed in the bathroom of their house. Bud attended the funeral and we all grieved upon his return. Grandpa Ben was seventy-five years old. Grandma Sophie, still young in spirit and energy, visited us often in Chicago after his death. But she felt lonely, despite doing her best to meet the demands of living alone. Bud and I considered the possibility of relocating her to Chicago to be near us, but she loved Texas and refused to move. She finally came to grips with being alone and managed beautifully, converting to an organic lifestyle. She bought all her groceries from an up-and-coming new Austin store called Whole Foods, where she equipped herself with their machinery and prepared her own combinations of high-fiber wheat and bran assortments. In addition, she consumed scores of vitamins, minerals, and fresh vegetables daily to keep her vitality level at an all-time high.

"She will live to be a hundred," Bud said repeatedly.

She was six years shy of his prediction. She died at ninety-four but only because she fell and declined. Actually, inactivity killed her.

Chapter 28

The 1970s brought many changes in our children. As teenagers in high school, the girls had many friends and participated in school activities. However, their Brownie and Girl Scout days came to an end, and their green scarves covered with badges turned into mementoes to store away in their memory boxes.

But David was a different story as he began to develop his first enthusiasms and hobbies. He got introduced to baseball through Little League when his friend Tommy signed up, then encouraged Dave to join.

"Come on, Dave. I know you'll like playing ball."

That seemed like an obvious guess, because David already loved the challenges of street baseball, hockey, basketball, and touch football. In wintertime, Bud froze over our kidney-shaped patio just so Dave and his friends could play hockey games, which often ran quite late on Friday nights. I enjoyed watching them from our kitchen window as they swirled and skated with excitement on the hardened ice. At night the patio lights went on and they started up again, whooshing a puck around after they cleared off all the furniture.

In summertime, they loved baseball. The kids either gathered on the streets or down at the park, playing any given time they had the chance. One day, Bud decided to take Dave shopping for a glove. Dave's eyes glowed as he conditioned the golden brown leather, and the treasured glove never left his side. Every time I looked at David, he seemed to be either tossing a ball into the air and catching it with his glove or swinging a bat in an imaginary practice.

So it came as no surprise when he asked, "Can I sign up for baseball, Mom?"

After the initial okay, there was no stopping him and we turned into his greatest fans. Coaches and owners saw his potential and even spoke of a scholarship possibility.

We held up family dinners every day until the game ended, and spent Saturdays and sometimes Sundays sitting on spectator's benches watching the game while baseball diamonds attracted players to run the fields regardless of the weather. Even cloudy skies and rain predictions didn't keep us home.

Moms and dads showed up for each game and friendships developed not only among the boys, but between parents also. Bud purchased a video camera and spent some games sitting in a tree getting the perfect picture.

It goes without saying that we felt extremely proud of our son as we watched him go through Little League, continue on through high school baseball, and pass the cuts for the American Legion semi-professional team as the fastest and most precise shortstop minor league baseball had ever seen. Even his coach remarked that David had the potential to be "one of the best shortstops to come out of high school." He possibly could have entered major league baseball, except he decided to take another route and return to college for his degree in journalism. A scholarship never came through for Dave, but his years as a professional, in his own mind, made the adventure worthwhile.

As we watched Dave enjoy his hour of fulfillment, we also watched our teenagers grow into adult women thinking courageously about college. Karen selected Illinois State and focused on a business degree.

"Dad has influenced me," she stated. Bud was an accountant who spent several years after our marriage attending evening classes at Illinois Institute of Technology to obtain his degree. He became her role model.

Kathy, on the other hand, sewed and loved fashions. She started her training at Harper Junior College and then moved on to Southern Illinois University in Carbondale, where she graduated with a degree in tailoring and design. I liked to think I influenced her because of the many hours spent teaching her how to sew as a youngster.

When Kathy went away to college, Misha, our Siberian Husky, missed her terribly, and now is a good time to tell about memories that will always remain with us.

Misha, given to Kathy in high school by Rob, her boyfriend, had lived with us since the age of nine weeks. As we nursed her back from mange and other ailments, she became a wonderful part of our family and learned to get along quite well with Terri, our feisty little terrier.

Missing Kathy, Misha turned to me for love and attention. I remember cold mornings in Chicago with the snow piled high in our backyard. There, curled up in a deep prepared hole, would be Misha. She slept outdoors nightly. When darkness descended, she'd find me, then sit and stare at me with her beautiful blue eyes.

Bending down, I'd say, "Misha, it's too cold to go out tonight."

But she'd run to the door, then turn back to see if I was coming. When outdoors, she'd sniff to find her spot, then circle many times before settling down for the night.

One morning, peering out our kitchen window, I saw a huge German Shepherd chasing her around the yard. At last, he trapped her and the deed was done. Then, he disappeared. I will never forget the look on her face when she came indoors. She acted like she felt dirty and destroyed.

I also felt destroyed, because I let her down. I had no

indication she was in heat, and wouldn't have allowed her "sleep outs" knowing this. So I gave her a bath and dried her gorgeous coat. As I covered her with a blanket, she licked my nose and I giggled.

Bud noticed the change in her. "Something's wrong with Misha," he remarked over his reading glasses one evening.

"Why?" I asked.

"She's listless and sleeping a lot," he answered.

I began to watch her more closely and realized finally that Misha was pregnant.

Before the puppies arrived, Bud built her a shelter in the shed, covered with straw for warmth when her time came. Then, he cut an opening in the lower part of the door so she and the puppies could come and go at will.

Upon searching for her one afternoon, we found her curled up in the straw, and we knew why. Bud checked periodically as I sat on a stool cringing with each contraction. I realized her pain, having been there myself.

Witnessing Misha's six beautiful puppies, part Shepherd and part Husky, come into the world was wonderful. She cleaned them, looking at me for my approval. As a family, watching Misha's puppies grow became a connecting time of our lives.

Since we had our other dog, Terri, and a small backyard, we decided to put all the puppies up for adoption. We advertised, placing three-by-five cards in grocery stores, restaurants, and K-Mart, plus a one-week ad in the local newspaper. The puppies found homes immediately—they were beautiful and went two at a time.

I then began working full time, and we all realized that Misha would not get the attention she needed. We called Kathy at school for a suggestion. She recommended calling her friend Rob in California. "He may want her," she said.

This suggestion appealed to us. Rob's mother lived nearby and we thought we might see Misha occasionally when he visited her, making it easier to part with this loving dog. We immediately called Rob.

"I'll take her, Mrs. Nardecchia. I could use the company," he answered. Rob was going to school and living alone.

Later trips to the airport always reminded us of Misha's frightened blue eyes that day as we placed her in the kennel, and our tearful eyes as we watched the plane ascend.

There's a happy ending, though. Rob returned periodically, bringing Misha to visit us. Then one day, he returned for good. He married our daughter, Kathy, and Misha remained in the family until she died at the age of twelve.

ଔ   ଔ   ଔ

During this time, Marie's family grew and married.

Johnny, hired for a California job, had a quick but glorious wedding to Cathy Kreuger, and we watched with awe the union of Jamie Zimardo and Gordan Heineiman, Frank and Florence's daughter and new son-in-law.

Anticipating another garden wedding, beautifully done with floral dresses and large hats, Bud decided that he too had to have proper attire with more emphasis and flair. I remembered the day he carried in a covered item from Marshall Field's and tucked it way back into his closet. While snooping, I found a white suit under the plastic protection—obviously he meant not to reveal his purchase until he had mustered the courage to wear it for a special occasion. It turned out weddings were the intended special occasion.

He first promenaded the suit at Philip's wedding, worn fashionably with a brown shirt and solid brown tie. He dazzled everyone at Tommy and Genean's wedding and then stole the show at Jamie's wedding as well. To his disappointment, Karen's and Kathy's weddings required tuxedoes, but the white suit materialized again at Michael and Mary's ceremony. Relatives dubbed him "The White Knight," "The Ice Cream Man," and even "Dr. Bud," but speaking as a prejudiced wife, all in all he was the handsomest fellow there.

Marie and Jack, finally finding contentment in their existence since Mom's death, began to enjoy life more. They traveled with Frank and Florence on cruises and saw the dawning of a new era when Heidi and Alexander were born to Philip and Crystel. Johnny and Cathy brought forth Christopher, and Cheryl, married to Dennis at the time, gave birth to Christant in September of 1974.

Life seemed simpler then, and we all accepted the everyday occurrences with loads of laughter sprinkled with tears.

Cheryl and Christiant

166

The Zimardo Family
Bruce, Christy, Tricia, and Cheryl
1994

Chapter 29

We loved our daughters" college years, especially all the events we attended where we had so much fun, but when the girls started bringing boyfriends home for our approval, it became serious business. Sometimes we thought...well, maybe. Another time—absolutely not. And one we will never forget—one well over six feet tall who seemed wildly out of scale with this lovely four-foot, ten-inch daughter of ours. We smiled through it all and prayed quietly.

Then in her junior year, a phone call from Illinois State gave me considerable thought when Karen said, "Mom, I've met someone really nice. He lives in Des Plaines.

Can I have him over for dinner when I come home this weekend?"

How can a mother say no? I thought Des Plaines wasn't too far, a suburb of Chicago, so why not?

The minute he walked through the door, I knew this was going to be serious business. Tim Barry was adorable—just her size, slim, good-looking, and so very pleasant. At first the beard bothered us, but we adjusted. Tim to this day will say he never felt too sure of how Bud felt about him. He was mistaken, because Bud saw a genuine young man who might take his first daughter away from him, and he approved. Tim is now a Certified Public Accountant who believes in working hard and strives to make life comfortable for his family.

With diligent minds and hands, Kathy and I put together a shower once Karen and Tim announced their engagement. Karen will probably never forget it, because our plan to surprise her worked so well. Tim took her camping and then suggested they stop by the house on the way home for him to talk to Bud about taxes. Karen was sweaty, badly in need of a shower, and dressed in short jeans. She was so concerned about her appearance, I thought surely she'd run and hide. But, being the trouper she is, the shower went off like a breeze and everybody had a great time.

When the big day came, melon dresses and baby breath bouquets beautified the bridesmaids, while the handsome groomsmen sported beige tuxedoes and melon boutonnières. St. Stephen's Church in Des Plaines opened its doors October 4, 1980, to all of us as Tim's friend Father Lefebre performed the nuptials.

We treasure the day we met all nine members of the Barry family. This lovely Irish brood of four girls and three boys, belonging to Gene and Peg Barry, brought another dimension to our lives. Now we had another family to consider for holidays, birthdays, and special occasions. Sharing our daughter with others was something we never had to do before, and we didn't always find that easy, but finally we realized that they in turn had to share their son with us. It became a pleasure to enjoy dinners, parties, and good times with our new in-laws.

Karen and Tim's wedding picture

Kathy, in the meantime, graduated from Southern Illinois University with a degree in design and tailoring and literally pounded the sidewalk for a job. She found retail a cloistered world—very hard to get into. Finally, after countless resumes and interviews, she got a job with a department store in downtown Chicago called Wieboldt's. She loved her job. They trained her for numerous departments and she eventually became manager of the jewelry department.

But her time there did not last. This wonderful Chicago store, dating back seventy-five long years or more, closed for good and Kathy lost her job. Starting over had to feel devastating for her, but she once again answered ads, applied to employment agencies, and pounded the sidewalks. A new Chicago store came into existence at this time called Main Street. She saw an ad in the paper requesting new employees. I could hear the typewriter clicking late at night as she again prepared resumes.

"I sent my resume in, Mom," she remarked one day.

"To whom?" I asked

"Main Street," she answered. "I'm bound and determined to get in there."

I'm not exaggerating when I say she literally called the office of that store every day for two weeks requesting an interview. I felt tempted so many times to say, "Kathy, give it a rest and try another store." But her determination made me a believer.

Exactly two weeks after her persistent campaign began, she got a new job and an old courtship resumed. While she learned her new job duties, an old love returned. I introduced Rob and Misha earlier in the story, but they deserve more recognition.

Our doorbell rang one warm sunny afternoon in June. Our front flowerbeds teemed with blooming petunias and summer's spectacular array surrounded us. I had just finished dressing a pork roast with lots of garlic, basil, and oregano for dinner. As the fragrant seasonings filled the air, I placed the roast in the oven and ran to answer the doorbell.

Through the screened front door I saw two familiar objects, both of whom I loved dearly. There stood a broad-smiling Rob Hughes and a beautiful Misha.

Rushing to open the door, I said gleefully, "Come in, come in."

I couldn't hug Misha enough. Rob evidently had just given her a bath and she glowed magnificently, with her bright blue eyes telling me she remembered me.

They both walked across the family room into the kitchen and we sat to chat. In his shorts and t-shirt, Rob brought a bit of California into our home and I couldn't refrain from hugging him also. As I handed him a glass of iced tea, I asked casually, "What are you doing in Palatine?"

"Visiting Mom," he answered.

"Oh, Misha looks divine," I remarked. "And so do you."

His dark hair and light eyes highlighted his huge frame, reminding me of his football years as a handsome champion.

After small talk and general conversation, Rob asked when Kathy would be home.

"She's always home for dinner," I told him.

After more hugs and kisses from me, they left and the phone rang that evening.

"Mrs. Nardecchia, this is Rob. Can I talk to Kathy, please?" He wasted no time in calling.

Pretending to have duties in the kitchen, I hung around waiting to see Kathy's reaction to the telephone call. She smiled a lot and definitely seemed interested, and I observed patiently as they began dating again.

Then, one evening as I sat looking out our sliding door, absorbed in the beauty of the budding trees and all the harbingers of spring, two glowing young people came through the garage door entrance leading into our family room.

Something seemed amiss, I thought. Bud wandered into the family room and my eye caught a sparkling diamond on Kathy's third finger, left hand.

Excitedly, I said, "What's going on here? What's that on your finger?"

The hugs and kisses came immediately and Kathy blushed with excitement. They decided to plan their wedding for the following September.

Again we approached this festivity with a cool head and a pounding heart. A shower brought Kathy's girlfriends, relatives, and old friends together. We selected wedding dresses and floral arrangements and Rob's mother, Delores, met all of family members. Rob's father had passed away some years before.

Kathy and I arranged a meeting with the Arlington Country Club in Arlington Heights for a reception, and together we expressed our preferences. With gracious cooperation from the Club, the staff carried out all our suggestions and requests. Blessed with a beautiful blue sky, a warm September day, and a stretch limousine fondly donated by United Rental Company, David's employer, Rob and Kathy became man and wife at St. Thomas of Villanova Church in Palatine. Misha, living with Rob's mother at the time, smiled with sparkling blue eyes as she rubbed and swayed her body around Kathy's legs. After their honeymoon, the couple made their home in Kansas City, Kansas.

Rob and Kathy's wedding picture

173

Chapter 30

A trip to the University of Wisconsin in June of 1980 excited our seventeen-year-old son about college. As we strolled the campus, his interest grew and he knew he wanted to attend this school. Many times in visiting Austin, Texas, Bud took us over to the University of Texas to explore the campus. David saw similarities in the two schools and immediately loved it.

Although the school accepted and he enrolled, he did not stay. While the country relived over and over again the shooting of President Ronald Reagan in 1981 by John Hinckley, Jr., David returned home. In that chaotic time, he felt uncertain of the path he wanted to follow. After much weighing of options, he attended Harper Junior College and then got a job working for a car rental company.

ଔ   ଔ   ଔ

By this time, God had blessed us with two granddaughters. Tim and Karen had Lisa and Kate and moved into a home in Hoffman Estates, Illinois. But this wasn't easy for them. They first had to sell a small home they owned in Carpentersville, Illinois. This troublesome home had a perpetually overflowing toilet due to extensive tree roots that had grown into the plumbing system. They had to spend large amounts of money on Roto-Rooter work and clearing up one mess after another.

On top of that, the home's location in a seedy neighborhood prevented it from selling right away. Poor response on the realtor's part didn't help, either. But finally after Tim and Karen took it off the market for a year and then placed it back on the following spring, the house sold. What a relief! As parents, Bud and I worried about our grandchildren growing up in that area anyway.

We felt not only relieved, but greatly honored when our children called and said, "Mom, we want you and Dad to see this house in Hoffman Estates."

One walk-through and we encouraged them.

"Grab it," we said.

The two-story house had three bedrooms and a full bath upstairs. The first floor featured a long foyer leading into the breakfast area, with a nice kitchen on the left of the breakfast area and a family room with a fireplace on the right. The house also had a parlor, a dining room, and a half bath downstairs. It was a marvelous house, crowned throughout with mahogany woodwork—and best of all, in their price range.

Surrounded by tall trees and healthy landscaping, the house sat in a beautiful neighborhood that bordered the affluent towns of Barrington and Inverness. What a prize! They were truly excited about their new place, After Tim and Karen moved in with furniture, bag, and baggage in September of 1986, the house took on a new splendor. With Dad's help, Karen wallpapered the kitchen, parlor, dining room, and half bath. Next they gave particular attention to polishing the hardwood floors and covering the windows with drapes. She and Tim did most of the work, with some more help from Tim's father, and the house grew into a thing of beauty, with a garden of flowers in the summertime and a glowing fireside of burning logs in the wintertime. What a magnificent accomplishment!

CR   CR   CR

1986 brought us another family wedding and the devastating news about the space shuttle Challenger exploding. Our space program was so successful until this disaster, and Americans wept with the loss of the brave astronauts. We all felt Christa McAuliffe's death, especially, as a huge blow because the tragedy doomed her hopes of relaying actual events to enthusiastic students.

Our latest family wedding brought us some much-welcomed happiness, not sorrow as Marie and Jack's last son, Michael, married Mary Borucki. We all delighted in this joyful wedding, which allowed families to get together again in camaraderie mixed with festivity and good food. The white suit won honors again, allowing tremendous opportunities for teasing Bud. Marie's boys never suppressed an opportunity to enjoy humor or laughter, always hoping to make someone the butt of their joke. All was done in good humor, though, and it added to the jovial exchanges between Joe, Frank, Jack, and Bud.

We will never walk this road again. Let us collect the best parts and box them for future memories.

Chapter 31

The years unfolded, but at some point Bud retired from Natural Gas Pipeline Company, alias Mid-Con Corporation, alias Occidental Gas Company, and became a stay-at-home Dad. What can I say? They offered him an excellent retirement package and at sixty-five, he felt ready. Approximately seven hundred employees in the company grabbed at the opportunity, allowing the new boss, Armand Hammer, to empty his desks economically.

Bud kept busy while staying home full-time, but his thoughts always returned to Texas. After a few years of shoveling Chicago snow and struggling with short-season gardening, he presented his case for leaving. With two daughters married and a twenty-one year-old son who we considered quite capable of taking care of himself, we gave serious thought to Bud's eighty-year-old-mother living alone and the notion of Bud returning to his roots.

Though not aware of all the adjustments involved, we returned to Austin, Texas several times to plan and coordinate the necessary elements, step by step.

First, I had to resign my job at Samuel A. Kirk Center, a school for disabled children. We had to sell our current house. Furthermore, we needed to come up with a practical plan for living in Austin: a new home, for one thing. We made several investigatory trips back and forth. Finally, through helpful friends in Austin, we located a realtor who found the exact home we had in mind up in the northwest corridor of Austin, where not too long ago deer roamed and miles of open land encouraged hunting. We found our new house in a thriving collection of newly built homes called Jester Estates.

Selling our precious little home in Palatine for twenty-five years turned out to be the hard part. We realized that moving meant leaving behind family, good neighbors, and heartbreaking memories. The hardest goodbyes would involve our daughter Karen, her family, and Jack and Marie. We also dreaded leaving behind many additional family members and friends, for we had many in both categories.

But we went through with our plan and put our house up for sale. The first interested buyer dropped out after finances became an issue. The house sat for a long time until our neighbor, who had just received her realtor license, picked it up off the list and sold it. We felt ever-grateful to her for that, but it didn't make leaving any easier. Explaining wasn't easy!

"Why are you going?" asked Marie.

"Bud hasn't gone home in a long time," I said. "He feels his mother needs help and security. It's the right thing to do." This explanation didn't help, either.

Finally, I stopped explaining and tearfully left in April 1988, to start a new life in a strange land. But a part of us came along— David decided to quit his job and relocate with us. He agreed to return to school in Texas and get his degree. Taking him along made it so much easier for me, enabling a broken heart to mend while I watched his continued growth. He graduated with honors from Southwest Texas State (now Texas State University) in journalism and communications.

Other family came down to visit, too. First Karen came with the two little girls. What a delight to have them for a whole month! Then, a welcome surprise occurred—Rob and Kathy were transferred from Kansas City to San Antonio. We viewed this too good to be true. They bought a home in a town called Cibolo about thirty-five miles south of Austin. Kathy and I spent endless time together sewing and draping windows.

After she arrived Kathy again searched for a job and became a Hallmark sales representative. Her job was to set up and remodel all the Walgreen's card departments in the Austin and San Antonio area. Proud of her responsibilities, she also had to hire her own crew.

"Mom and Dad, how would you feel about working for me?" she asked one warm but rainy afternoon. She had just arrived from her usual hour-long ride from San Antonio.

"What do you mean?"

"I need to assemble my own working crew and thought you might be interested."

We had accomplished all our goals for the new house and welcomed the prospect of a productive outlet, so we agreed. Every morning we trudged off to work with her, collecting all the newly arrived Minnesota ladies on the block to assist. After the 3M Company transferred a group of employees to Austin from Minnesota, a number of them moved in on our block and became our good friends. Helen W., Linda, Billie, Jan, and sometimes Carmie all joined Kathy's crew willingly and worked cooperatively until our team restructured practically every Walgreen's store in the vicinity.

We spent endless hours on our knees cleaning storage bins, sorting cards, and installing new fixtures. We felt so proud of Kathy's aptitude and the exactness she displayed each day as she demanded perfection with a kind heart. We'd drag home each night dirty and exhausted, but up and willing to go again the next morning. Some of us found steady jobs with Walgreen's as card managers after she left her job. Being part of this rewarding experience helped my loneliness and led to enjoyable new friendships.

My spirits rose even higher with our next bit of family news. What better news can one receive than to hear about a new baby on its way? To our delight, Kathy was pregnant.

As Bud prepared a barbecue brisket with corn on the cob and spicy beans one evening, our excitement escalated over cocktails when family conversation turned to a new baby.

"And what will you name this child?" I asked.

"What do you suggest?" responded Kathy.

We laughed at different ideas, eliminating Sabitino right at the very start, and not even a thought crossed their minds to say

"Helen." Then, very quietly, Rob said, "Sam." Now, in 1992, Sam was not an overwhelming popular name. There were Todds, Bryans, Ryans, and Jasons, but not too many Sams at the time. Even though it was Buddy's brother's name, we weren't too sure, but after Bud and I rolled the name around in our heads a few times we agreed it had possibility. A girl would definitely be Emily. That we liked right away.

After a surprise shower in our new family room with several friends on the block and some old acquaintances, Samuel Hughes was born August 1, 1992 sharing his birth date with our granddaughter Lisa.

Sam's huge head scared us. The doctor worried and ordered several X-rays and brain scans to make sure he was fine. With thanks to God, Sam was fine, but it took a Caesarian section to bring him into the world.

Kathy resigned as a Hallmark representative, but Walgreen hired three workers of her crew to work in their stores. I was one, maintaining the card department for six years before I retired.

A little while after Kathy left her job, a surprise letter arrived from Marie. Bud and I were planting rows of flowers on a blustery, warm March day when the mailman jammed our box with various pieces of unwanted mail. Walking across the street to retrieve it, my eye caught the corner post office stamp that indicated Chicago.

Excitedly, I opened the envelope with a soiled hand and read as Bud dug holes and planted impatiens.

"They're coming!" I shouted.

He looked up with surprise as I watched his hair blow around his forehead.

"Who's coming?" he asked.

"Marie, Jack, Frank, and Florence." I was jubilant.

Up to this time, I always went back and forth to Chicago for all family visits. Sometimes, Bud went. Other times he didn't. But never had the family visited us. I had ample reason to feel jubilant.

The house, even though brand new, had to be put in immaculate order to suit me. After we planted, cleaned, prepared beds, pre-cooked some meals, and stocked the liquor cabinet, we waited to welcome our guests with open arms.

The glorious part was the good health we all enjoyed at the time. Jack had his usual doctor appointments with careful examinations of his heart, which wasn't always tip-top since his bypass years before. But overall, we all had plenty of energy to enjoy each other and have a good time.

Frankie and Roslyn, 1990

Bud happily created lasagna, roasts, steaks, barbeque, Mexican food, and so much more at each and every meal. We prefaced each meal with cocktail time and luscious appetizers on our large redwood deck. The week flew by.

"Do you really have to go?" I asked when it all ended. We

rode in silence to Robert Mueller Airport and tearfully waved goodbye. I prayed they'd come another day soon.

Instead, anxiety ripped our hearts in October of 1992, when Frankie collapsed at a file cabinet in his office and was rushed to the hospital. In his seventies now, Frank showed no signs of weakening. His lifelong good looks stayed with him through the years as well as his frolicking good nature. We were at a loss to know what caused his collapse.

Doctors worked for hours trying to correct the cerebral hemorrhage that had attacked his brain. Frank emerged from the surgery a different person, with thought and speech patterns so damaged that others found his jumbled verbal phrases difficult to understand. Trying hard to get a complete sentence out became stressful for him.

The first year his vocabulary was affected. However, he had a great spirit and tried so hard to improve his memory, but unfortunately he suffered more bleeds in the brain. As Florence will tell you, no one ever tried harder to improve. His speech and cognitive therapists just loved him, and his efforts amazed them. In spite of it all, he could still make them laugh.

On our next visit to Chicago, Buddy and I spent time with Frank trying desperately to make sense of his conversations. The doctors told the family that they removed a clot the size of a fist from the area of his brain that handles vision, speech, and processing of thoughts. Although Frank thought he was saying a coherent sentence, the words got reversed and the sentences came out all jumbled. We all had difficulty understanding him.

Our drive home to Texas was quiet, extending sometimes into miles of silence; Buddy and I wondering how long he could live like that. The decline was slow, the future unpredictable.

At first, there were encouraging signs. His energy level seemed normal, his appetite good. Although he had difficulty responding to a conversational topic, he could hear and absorb. Over the period of the first good year, the family thought they noticed signs of improvement. Frank attended occupational therapy for quite some time, which helped up to a certain point, but the following year brought on dementia and more difficult times.

"He will lick this," I can remember thinking. "He's that hardy little boy who rode his bicycle delivering the morning newspapers in below-zero weather, the kid who dragged a Christmas tree up two flights of stairs to show Mom and made our Thanksgiving joyous because of a turkey we didn't think we'd have. This is Frank, he'll come through this."

But God knew it wasn't meant to be.

Chapter 32

As we worried and prayed for Frank, 1993 brought other surprises. Our "across the street" neighbors, Jim and Helen, turned into good friends and we sipped wine and ate dinners together often. Jim, a semi-retired 3M salesman, and his wife, Helen, a retiree's wife like me, both had graying or white hair with sparkling eyes and tender smiles. Jim referred to us as Helen 1 and Helen 2. We often questioned who came first.

Bud and I talked about visiting Rome more than once, but we needed a push or shove to arrange plans and go. As a globe-trotting salesman, Jim had traveled back and forth to different parts of the world and had seen the splendor of Italy on many occasions. He gave us the push and shove we needed to make a dream come true.

The four of us made travel arrangements and in March of 1993, Delta Airlines took us on our journey. Since Jim was combining business with pleasure, he and Helen sat in First Class while we sat in Coach. But a layover in New York changed that, making several empty seats available in First Class. Imagine our delight when the flight crew invited us to sit with Jim and Helen in the First Class section. They treated us royally and we loved every moment of it.

Our arrival in Rome after fourteen hours of flying time deserved rejoicing and we took a cab to Hotel Delta, within walking distance to the Coliseum and the Roman Forum. The first thing Buddy did was look up all the Nardecchias in the phone book, hoping to find one just down the street. He spotted several but he picked the one that seemed closest to our location and called.

With a little luck, he located a Theresa Nardecchia, who owned a small store, but communicating by phone didn't work out too well. Based on the address, however, Bud decided that the store couldn't be too far, so he devised a plan to find it. Bud was determined.

Our first day was sensational as we dodged mopeds flying down the main street at top speed. We never could figure out rhyme or reason to traffic lights or rules. I don't think there were any. No one seemed to observe any, but top speed was the goal.

After walking around to take in a few of the sights, we returned to our hotel. The doors in our rooms opened up to a veranda that invited seating while the smells of Rome swirled all around us. We sipped wine and then made our way to a small restaurant down the street for dinner called Trattoria's. The aroma of veal Parmesan, olive oil, and fresh basil caused our heads to swirl and our breath to whoosh. We sat in a booth as an authentic Italian waiter, who looked the part in a white shirt complemented with a black bow tie and white apron, walked our way. We watched as he removed the long white napkin hanging on his arm to dust off the red and white checked tablecloth. He skillfully handed us a menu. Smiling was not part of his job.

I think I can recall Jim, Helen, and I ordering veal Parmesan, but Bud wanted to order something different and settled on a dish calling for stewed tomatoes and tripe. He regrets that to this day.

We slept well that night and eagerly anticipated morning.

We spent the second day of our nine-day dream touring the Coliseum. As we made our way through the jam-packed arena, we imagined gladiators preparing for the fight of their lives in front of forty-five or fifty thousand people. The seating capacity for this creation was massive. The collection of broken stones and piled-high rocks told endless stories without saying a word. We stepped back from the iron cages as though ferocious wild lions would attack.

Bud brought forth a glass bottle he had carried with him from Austin and spooned Coliseum soil into the bottle as a memento of this miraculous land. But eight more days stretched before us with so much more to see.

The next day we decided to explore the Coliseum in more detail and take lots of photographs. From there we visited the Arch of Constantine and then decided to cross Via dei Fori Imperiali to explore The Roman Forum. Our brochure told us that the Roman Forum formed the literal heart of Roman history—it once served as the center for trade, religion, and politics. The extraordinary stone figures of the Vestal Virgins, that group of privileged women who watched the sacred fire, symbolic of the life of Rome, created lasting mental images of courage and resilience.

After gathering our strength, we headed up The Palatine Hill, which led us to the first monumental palaces that formed the city of Rome. At this point in time, we felt we had seen the best of Rome, but we had not. Much more remained.

As Rome had its customs, so did we. After long walks and hours of exhilaration, we found our way back to our hotel for relaxation, but not without an antipasto served with great tastes of Chianti or another of Italy's fine wines. As we roamed in Rome we found an Italian grocery store we insisted on calling Giuseppe's. When we stepped in, my mind flew back to my beginnings on Taylor Street where succulent aromas of olive oil, Parmesan cheese, and garlic permeated the air. Giuseppe's went a step further with the wafting smell of fresh baked bread.

It goes without saying that Bud was in his glory as he asked for an assortment of this cheese and that cheese complemented with pepperoni, hot peppers, and black olives.

"Could you please cut the bread a bit thinner?" Bud asked.

However, Guiseppe never quite got the bread thin enough to suit Bud, so after several trips to our favorite grocery store, Guiseppe finally invited Bud to come behind the counter to cut his own. And he did!

This formed our ritual after each day of exploring and discovering the wonders of Rome: Giuseppe's first, then back to the hotel for our veranda gathering with delectable antipasto and wine. A late dinner followed at a nearby trattoria, and then a deep sleep.

We set aside the third day of our Roman adventure designated to track down the Nardecchia family, who owned a store in the northern most part of Rome. With a map of Rome and Jim for our guide, we couldn't go wrong. We started out with confidence on our walk, stopping occasionally to regroup and rest.

"Buddy, I think we need to study this map again,"

Jim said a few times after a long, tiring walk that seemed to lead nowhere. We can honestly say we saw a lot of Rome that day. And then, wait—there it is—NARDECCHIA'S, read a sign above a small store on a side street. With great relief, we entered.

Two men worked diligently behind a counter doling out delicious-looking beef and sausage sandwiches topped with green peppers and onions, then served on crusty Italian bread. They also added sliced mozzarella, provolone, and black olives on request. Our mouths watered as we watched the clerks prepare the succulent treats.

But clearly, we had a slight problem as no one spoke English. We struggled in vain to communicate until the bell tinkled on the door and a well-dressed man walked in wearing a fedora. He heard Bud saying, "I am a Nardecchia. The owner is a Nardecchia. I've come from America to meet her."

The men behind the counter nodded their heads up and down and said, "Nardecchia, ya, ya." But they didn't understand. By this time, Jim and Helen had walked outdoors so other customers could enter the small store.

Finally, the man with the fedora stepped forward and said, "I speak English and Italian. Maybe, I can help you."

He was heaven-sent.

"Tell them my name is Sabitino Nardecchia. My father's name was Benedetto. We live in Texas. We may be related to the owner."

The man with the fedora spoke fluent Italian. In the beautiful sounds of the Italian language, he apparently got the message through and one of the gentlemen reached for the phone and dialed a number.

Turning to us, the man with the fedora said, "The owner, Theresa Nardecchia, is very old, over ninety, but they are calling her to see if she will speak to you."

The conversation went quickly between them, but she refused to talk to Bud. We left disappointed and hailed a cab. We longed for our veranda retreat, dinner, and a good night sleep.

The following days were filled with the Papacy of Rome. We entered St. Peter's Basilica, where the Papal Palace has housed popes for centuries. It's hard to do anything but gasp at the size and magnificence. Take a slight turn to the right and in a small chapel on a far wall you will find Michelangelo's Pieta. I could not look on this magnificent sculpture without tears. I wanted to touch the limp hand of Jesus that hung to the marble floor, but it is screened off for protection from unwanted tourists who have damaged it in the past.

An early bus took us to the Vatican Museums and the Sistine Chapel the next day. The Vatican runs a bus service between St. Peter's Square and the upper entrance of the museums. It's impossible to visit the many museums all in one day, but the handsomely decorated buildings leave a lasting impression.

We found the Sunday we spent at the Sistine Chapel particularly rewarding. Dressed for a Mass celebration, we joined thousands of people in St. Peter's Square. There we discovered the Mass was being said by His Holiness himself, Pope John Paul II, a reward we did not anticipate. The canonization Mass celebrated a Spanish priest who had died glorifying Christ in the 1800s.

Bud and I literally fought our way to the front for snapshots of our Pope. The crowd seemed calm and quiet, but pushy. I found myself wrapped around a large column yards from His Holiness, who sat on a throne high up on the altar wearing a miter. I snapped only a couple of shots as the crowd pushed and demanded space. Bud followed on my heels, but we decided to leave before we totally lost Jim and Helen in the bedlam.

Then we waited in St. Peter's Square as the window of the Pope's apartment opened for his message of the day. Of course, he spoke in Italian, but it was such a glorious experience for Bud and me, both raised on Catholic doctrine from early childhood. We will never forget it.

The Sistine Chapel is a marvel in itself. According to

brochures and literature we picked up while touring, it took Michelangelo four and a half years to paint the beautiful ceiling of the chapel. Throngs of visitors walk around bumping into one another while looking up, trying to imagine the degree of stress and pressure placed on Michelangelo in completing this magnificent work. In the end, he not only did the ceiling but the Last Judgment on the altar wall. His massive endurance was unimaginable considering the position in which he painted and the impairment of his sight.

Finding all the side benches filled in the Sistine Chapel prompted us to leave and get away from the crowd after we had explored the brilliance of this masterpiece. We opted for the Vatican Gardens and the carefully tended Borghese Gardens, both of which displayed brilliantly colored flowers, massive oak trees, and ancient fountains.

We then decided to return to our reverie of wine and antipasto so we made our way back to the hotel, after a stop at Giuseppi's, full of anticipation and enthusiasm for another day.

A cafeteria breakfast at the hotel and generally a pizza at a sidewalk cafe sufficed for our long walks or bus rides to our chosen sights. The following day, we ventured on and eventually found ourselves sitting on the Spanish Steps, where the many flights are filled with a wide variety of flowers. The warm sun greeted us as we stretched our legs on the landings. Supposedly, the fountain at the foot of the stairs has the sweetest water in Rome. We enjoyed watching the parents lift their children up to catch the thick jets of pure mountain water.

Next we found our way to the Fontana Di Trevi, which derived its popularity from the movie Three Coins in the Fountain, and of course, we tossed our coins in for the traditional good luck that's predicted. Based on the crowds we saw there, it's easy to guess why it's a must on everybody's itinerary.

After several days, we rested and discussed our remaining time in Italy. We decided to discontinue roaming Rome and explore the islands and gondolas of Venice instead. We wandered off to our sleeping quarters that night full of eagerness for the next day.

Right after breakfast the next day we checked the train schedule to find out how to get from Rome to the Santa Lucia Station. From the Santa Lucia Station we needed to catch a waterbus, also called a *vaporetto*, which would take us down the Grand Canal to San Marco in Venice. Thank goodness for the brochures and literature we collected on the way and saved. They have helped tremendously to refresh my memory on the different names and places that we encountered.

Our train tickets in hand, we rushed back to Hotel Delta to pack a bag. Not schooled in how to pack lightly, I became public enemy No. 1 when Jim and Bud had to carry my overstuffed overnight bag. One incident that I will always remember was the little delinquent who tried to pull Jim's camera from his shoulder as we descended the stairs to exit the station. As he stood next to a woman holding a baby, she actually encouraged him to steal. I found this not only scary, but heartbreaking.

With friends in Rome

On our waterway trip, we passed a beautiful church called San Simeone Piccolo just to the right of the railway station. The church dominates the whole first stretch of the Grand Canal. The Canal offers a continuous stretch of one church masterpiece after another, but the heart of the city is St. Mark's Square, which is awash with pigeons and tourists.

Our first mission was to find the Concordia Hotel, which turned out to be relatively easy since it overlooked St. Mark's Square. A Minnesota friend in Texas who had stayed there several years ago recommended The Concordia to us. We loved the décor of our rooms, designed softly in floral wallpaper with matching drapes and bedspreads. A booth hugged one of the walls where we sat for breakfast and consumed assorted refreshments with contentment and pleasure. Veranda doors opened up to the rooftops of houses that overlooked St. Mark's Square. Despite missing Guiseppe, we continued our search for wine and antipasto in Venice. However, the big thrill for me was sitting at small round tables in St. Mark's Square sipping wine while cameras clicked, pigeons swarmed all around, and people smiled a lot.

We tried, of course, to stamp all these images into our brains to hold and never forget, but after many years too much is forgotten and the urge to go back beckons.

On the plane coming home we each had our own silence, our own personal remembrances. Even now, I retrieve cherished memories from my mental "Favorite Places" folder, and a smile crosses my lips as places, words, and faces surface now ten years later. Like the young girl who sat next to me on the plane to Chicago.

"I love your glasses," she said in her Italian accent. "We wear a lot of the large frames in Italy."

My heart skipped a beat.

Chapter 33

As parents, my siblings and I felt comfortable and secure that we had launched our children safely on their way into life with the best foundation we could give them. Frank and Florence's daughter, Cheryl, lived in California until the earthquakes became too frequent, and then relocated to Oregon. By this time, she had two girls, Christy and Trisha. Frank and Florence's second girl, Jamie, had a good marriage with a strong young man and together they parented two children, Eric and Roslyn. Frank's son, Bruce, never left the homestead and worked diligently with Frank in his insurance business. With the rebellion of our American youth in the 60s and 70s, we all felt pleased that our children stayed close to home stable and sensible.

Marie's four sons were all married now, supporting and rearing their own families, so the only unattached member in the Zimardo collection of grandchildren was David, our son.

After earning his degree in journalism and communications from Southwest Texas State University, David worked at several different companies—some good, others not so good, but we looked upon them as stepping stones to a final career. He loved our home and everything about Texas.

David also brought home numerous girlfriends for our approval. He never said that, but we sensed that possibility. Now that he had entered his late twenties, he wanted a home and children of his own.

As we did with the young suitors the girls brought home, we shared our analysis of each girl David introduced. "Too chatty," Dad called one. "Too loud," I decided about another. And Dad's final opinion of the third one: "Too tall." But one evening around ten o'clock, the front door opened and David walked in with a very charming young lady. My eye immediately caught the curly dark red hair and the broad smile.

"Mom," he said sheepishly. "This is Margaret."

He had showed me a picture of Margaret a few days earlier and I remember saying, "Now this is the kind of girl I like," not knowing who she was or where she came from. They worked for the same company and had taken business trips together. Evidently, the time together sealed the relationship.

We then learned her last name was Mulligan and she was Irish and German, very pretty, and intent on making a good impression. I liked her immediately. Bud always took his time deciding who he liked or disliked, but with time he realized she was a good match for Dave. But the important thing was David loved her.

We never doubted that a wedding would ensue, so we felt little surprise when Margaret displayed her engagement ring one late afternoon in our breakfast area. Though pleased, we also felt a bit saddened. My mind rushed back to the many good times Dave, Bud, and I shared through the years: the trips we took together, the laughter we enjoyed, and the Chicago Cubs game we loved to analyze.

From Rick Sutclif to Sammy Sosa, we were die-hard Cub fans, and David taught me everything I needed to know. I often called him at work to tell him the Cubs won, and he alerted me to watch out for a tremendous new player who would steal the pitcher scene in the coming year.

"Mom, watch the game. Kerry Wood from Texas is pitching and he's outstanding."

And Kerry Wood was outstanding, striking out nine batters at his first attempt.

But all good things must come to an end, and Dave needed a home of his own filled with a loving wife and beautiful children. Margaret could give him this and we accepted her with open arms. I'm so glad we did, as she turned into a sweet addition to our family.

We planned a shower first and then a wedding. Becoming acquainted with Margaret's parents, Ed and Beverly Mulligan, was a bonus because we clicked immediately. Being pretty close to the same age, we found we had a lot in common and freely shared spirited conversation and camaraderie.

I felt ever so excited as we hung lavender bows all over the deck and trees in the backyard, cleared out the shed to serve as our bar, and placed long tables covered with lavender tablecloths around the yard for seating.

Ah, but the wedding ceremony stole the show as we trooped up the brick stairs to Mount Bonnell overlooking Lake Austin. On February 26, 1994, one of the coldest days of the year, David and Margaret said, "I do" before friends and relatives. Margaret, beautiful in her mother's white dress and veil from 1951, glowed as she held a bouquet of purple anemone and buttercup. David looked snappy in a black tuxedo. Everyone else froze and covered up with scarves and gloves.

No one in the Midwest imagines that Texans ever need to bundle up because of a frost or chilling wind that freezes faces and toes. We do, but only for a short time and then flowers bloom again and spring brightens our world.

We mustn't forget about guests. Our daughters and their families arrived from Chicago and Kansas City. Kathy was pregnant with Emily, their second child, who we soon cherished as our beautiful little granddaughter. Buddy's family came from Fort Worth and Batesville. Grandma Sophie also put in a short appearance, while many friends of David and Margaret's showed up. Three of David's high school buddies came from other states just to wish him their best. The joy of all of us gathering together made the preparations worthwhile. Everyone stood in line as the aroma of hot lasagna tickled their nostrils, and a large ham puffed out its chest on a silver tray. The beautifully displayed casseroles, salads, Jell-O molds, and desserts in the decorated garage shouted out for guests to taste them. And taste they did. Bud outdid himself and everyone noticed and complimented him on his specialties.

"Who did all this?" was the general question that circled the backyard. Bud and I just smiled, remembering all the wonderful parties and weddings we had served in the past. Memories are made of this!

Chapter 34

The day before David and Margaret's wedding, our phone rang. Buzzing around with preparation on my mind took up my entire concentration, eliminating any thought of who might be phoning.

"Get that will you, Bud?" I shouted from the dining room where I polished silverware and dragged out trays, platters, and serving pieces.

"Hi, Marie," Bud exclaimed jubilantly. "We're hard at it here bringing it all together. We'd love to have you and Jack arrive. It would make the party complete."

I polished excitedly, waiting to talk to her.

"Marie," I finally got to say. "It's good to hear from you. We're busier than a one-arm paperhanger."

Joking and laughing usually filled our conversations, but today I detected the nervousness in her voice.

"We can't come, Helen. Jack's not well. He's got to have a pacemaker put in to regulate his heartbeat. He's been very tired lately and his breathing's not good."

She didn't need to explain further. Jack's health was becoming a priority more and more as time went on. I felt sad because it meant the first family wedding without them. But the miles between created that. I told her I understood, and my tears came after we talked.

Marie watched Jack closely and their love continued strong. Each time Jack faltered, Marie explored and found a remedy.

196

Maybe a new doctor, a new medicine, a stay in the hospital to reinforce his strength, or even another surgery to put him back on the road to recovery. It worked every time. He'd pop back and begin all over again. He had had bypass surgery, prostate surgery, carpal tunnel syndrome correction, and numerous other procedures to improve the quality of his life. We missed them at the wedding but they were in our thoughts.

He came through all of them smiling. We'd kid by saying Jack had nine lives. We all loved this fair-haired, delightful man, so jovial and fun-loving, and we hoped for another quick recovery.

In 1995, we attended a wedding in Chappell Hill near Brenham, Texas between two of our son's young friends. The bride was Mr. Yong's daughter, and Mr. Yong was the Secretary-General of the Asia-Pacific Golf Confederation. He refereed and traveled with the International Tournament Tour. Through conversation with Mr. Yong at the wedding, Bud expressed how much he longed to see The British Open in Scotland. As it turns out, Mr. Yong was in charge of making reservations for tourists and he had four available openings. If we were truly interested, he offered to send us all the required information. Bud said, "Oh, we're interested, all right."

Also in that same year, we saw quite a bit of Beverly and Ed Mulligan, Margaret's parents. The conversation more than once centered around golf, since Bud and Ed both played the game regularly.

When Ed heard about the opportunity, he said, "Let's plan it."

Ed took over all the details and we left in July, beaming with excitement. This would be another fabulous memory, like Rome and Venice, something we would never forget. We flew Delta Airlines again and made flight connections with Ed and Bev in Atlanta. Hugs came when we saw one another and all four of us realized the thrill of the journey before us as we transferred flights to leave the good old USA on July 15th.

Bud's dream came true when we arrived in London Gatwick and picked up our Hertz car at Glasgow Airport on July 16th. We stayed overnight at the Swallow Hotel in East Kilbride, Scotland.

The next morning we woke up excited and eager to go as we drove to Edinburgh and toured the Edinburgh Castle, as well as the city. Crowds of people grouped around tour guides who told us all about medieval times and their heroes.

We spent July 18th touring the Highlands near Loch Ness and Inverness, a daylong tour of over 300 miles. Some of it can be very slow. Breathtaking greens, blues, yellows, and reds surrounded us as we drove along the Highlands, spotting the grazing sheep with their black faces. We stopped often to view God's beauty, taking pictures along the way.

We spent the next week at St. Andrews University, where we dined, slept, and walked to The Open every day thanks to the gracious efforts of Mr. Yong, who arranged our stay. We thrilled at the chance to watch professional golf played at its best under cloudy skies and cool temperatures. After a week of watching the greats, such as Nick Faldo, Arnold Palmer, Jack Nicklaus, and Ben Crenshaw, our excitement soared as John Daly became the first American to win the British Open since 1989. And we watched as a St. Andrews University student ran across the course from the gallery to give Nick Faldo a hug and a kiss. It was indeed a surprise to everyone, especially Nick Faldo.

Were Ed and Bud excited when Mr. Yong invited them to tour the Royal & Ancient Golf Club of St. Andrews building, take home a bottle of single malt liquor (which we still have, unopened), and view the inside of the front window where all the professional golfers congregate near the first tee? You bet! Bev and I were not allowed in the building— this was strictly a male domain. The Book of Rules read as follows:

The United States Golf Association and the Royal and Ancient Golf Club of St. Andrews will continue their close liaison in all matters concerning the Rules and their respective and mutual efforts to preserve and enhance the integrity of the game and its Rules. Both organizations would like to record their appreciation of the valuable assistance which

198

they have received from other golfing bodies throughout the world.

We enjoyed wonderful days over there and saw numerous castles while driving down the East Coast to the North Sea coast, where we found the castle at Bamburgh. Then we moved on to Alnwick to visit its castle, the current home of the Dukes of Northumberland.

Our rented car took us everywhere and Ed, was proficient in driving a foreign car with the steering wheel on the right, handling the car capably even on the narrow roads in the Highlands, where a bus can greet you coming around the corner. After several small towns and pubs, we drove to Stratford-on-Avon and stayed overnight at the Shakespeare Hotel. We always enjoyed the delicious and plentiful breakfasts at the hotels, but our favorite thing to do was walk the streets and have a pub lunch. The pub atmosphere and pub food never disappointed us, and our spirits lifted every time we walked through another pub door.

By the time Wednesday, July 26th rolled around, we realized the end was not too far off. We drove to Oxford, which dates from the 1400s, and then forty-five miles more on to Windsor. There we visited the castle, a cathedral, and Eton College, relishing this priceless roam through medieval history.

We arrived in London two days before our departure for home. Temperatures soared into the 90s—a rare weather phenomenon in London which is usually cool and damp with an almost absolute certainty of rain in the forecast. Scanning my wardrobe for cooler clothes reduced me to one pair of shorts and a short-sleeved silk blouse, which I washed out at night and put back on in the morning still damp and clammy. Our first night at the Chesterfield Hotel surprised us with no air conditioning or fans, and a humidity of nearly 100. We found it impossible to sleep. I remember looking at rooftops most of the night next to a window that only let in hot, humid air.

But when morning arrived, our dream itinerary provided a full schedule of events that kept the heat from overpowering us. We saw Parliament, Buckingham Palace, Big Ben, the glorious crowd pleaser known as the Changing of the Guard,

Westminster Abbey, Hyde Park, and Green Park, where we stretched out in chairs and listened to a band assembled on a gazebo. We saw tourists all over as we found Piccadilly Circus and the British Museum, climaxing the end of a day filled with English history, beautiful flower arrangements, and smiling Londoners who graciously entertained us. We will always remember Mrs. Brenner, who invited us into her home after she saw us admiring her front garden. Her great joy was showing us pictures of her family.

With friends in Scotland

Englanders put all of their hard work into front gardens because some don't have backyards. The hanging baskets dangling next to their front doors bloomed exquisitely with petunias, impatiens, and garden-fresh floral arrangements.

We will also remember eighty-year-old Carrie, who sat in a

pub evenings talking to strangers to keep her life interesting and prevent loneliness. We chatted with her on several occasions and returned because we found her so delightful and informative.

But like all good things, our trip had to come to an end and we left Gatwick on July 31st on Delta Flight 11 at 11:00 in the morning, filled with memories of great expectations. Will we return again? Probably not. But we stored lasting memories that pop back into our minds over and over again.

Chapter 35

Tired after our return home, we welcomed the sight of our familiar surroundings. After catching up on sleep and unpacking, my mind returned to Frank. Wondering how we'd find him, I called Florence. She told me she now had to hire caregivers to hold his hands and walk him around, even wheelchair him outdoors to sit in the sun in his jacket and cap. Family visited often, but he never improved—just declined. His heart attack years earlier and his constant smoking had thinned the arteries in his brain, causing mild tremors and mini-strokes. He was going downhill quickly.

As the years went on, he returned to the hospital more frequently until finally he was bedridden with no energy or endurance to continue, but still he lingered. Florence gave him her all.

Then, one afternoon around 5:00, the phone rang. Bud answered. I stood at the counter cutting up a salad, and his look as he handed me the phone told what I didn't want to hear. It was Marie.

"He's gone, Helen." I broke down. We realized it was for the best, since he couldn't live much longer in a vegetative state, but hearing the actual finality proved hard to endure.

After I hung up, Bud hugged me as I sobbed convulsively.

The solemn plane ride seemed to take forever. Our daughter, Karen picked us up at the airport and together we all attended the visitation and funeral. It poured down rain on a Saturday in November of 1997, and most of us felt grateful there would be no gravesite ceremony, since Frank was cremated. Reflecting back, I can see clearly the urn on a pedestal standing near the altar. Drooping and weeping, we filed out of church into the pouring rain. Some snow had mixed with rain and the overcast skies matched our mood as we jumped puddles to slip into cars. We will miss Frank always. His carefree behavior, handsome face, and generous heart will haunt our dreams.

His Mass card said it all:

> *God saw you getting weary,*
> *He did what He thought best;*
> *He put His arms around you*
> *And said, "Come and rest."*
> *He opened up His golden gates*
> *On that heartbreaking day,*
> *And with His arms around you*
> *You gently slipped away.*
> *It broke our hearts to lose you*
> *You did not go alone;*
> *A part of us went with you*
> *The day God called you home.*

Frank P. Zimardo, a United States Marine Corps veteran of World War II, fought his last battle courageously.

Years change things, and hearts heal slowly over time. We in Texas slowly got used to completing each day without Frank, while family in Chicago struggled to resume their normal activities. Frank's son-in-law, Gordon, took over the insurance business and kept it afloat, and runs it still to this day.

The 90s slipped away from us as the year 2000 peeked around the corner. 1999 brought a huge change in our lives and an opportunity that needed pursuing. When some friends from Minnesota who had once lived near us in Jester Estates came over for dinner, they talked about a retirement unit in a quaint town north of Austin called Georgetown. They had already put a down payment on a lot of their choice and invited us to visit when we came to the area. We accepted.

At River Bend Village II we found a retirement center that provided individual homes, not condos or townhouses, and we liked that idea. As we rode around and down Melissa Court I remember Dennis and Jan pointing out a site.

"That's our lot over there. The whole court will have white stone brick." It looked lovely and we were impressed. But only a couple of lots remained available.

One apparently undesirable lot stood on the corner of Stacey and Bootys Road; no one seemed to want it because it had a huge electrical transmitter at the far corner of the lot, complete with extensive wiring. The builder offered it to us at a five-thousand-dollar discount. After some very serious thought, we finally took it. Bud mentally mapped out how he planned to camouflage the high transmitter.

"We'll put a shed in front of it, " he said. "The trees are young and will cover it with time."

Well, it isn't completely covered but it's less obvious to us now, and we've learned to live with it. The landscaping and several gardens that Bud created look so beautiful that we hope no one notices the transmitter now five years later.

After we got serious about building in Georgetown, we drove there each weekend and got acquainted with the residents on Stacey Lane. We loved the layout of one model in particular. When various couples invited us in we saw the changes we could make to enlarge and create the house we desired. The great room needed expanding—our plan included this as well as a screened-in back porch. It would be lovely, we knew, and we moved closer to a decision.

Bud and I talked constantly about our present home being too large for us now that David was married. We also wanted to avoid second-floor bedrooms, especially since I suffered a great deal at that time with arthritis. Other problems with the house began to bother Bud and finally we made the decision to sell and move. It was one of the best decisions we ever made.

Moving to a smaller house meant a lot of items had to go, so we organized a big garage sale. Two tiring days of pricing and selling took its toll on us, but once we finally got through it we left and never looked back.

We have been in Georgetown for five years now, enjoying our new one-story home with its three bedrooms and two baths. We've accumulated new friends around our age whose company delights us. Neighbors entertain us and we entertain them, keeping the friendship flowing continuously. And as family comes to visit, the joy and laughter of children's voices has filled our home over and over again.

At a family wedding in 2000

Chapter 36

Not long after we moved, perhaps a year or so later, our daughter Kathy, with her husband Rob and two children, Sam and Emily, finally established in Colorado, decided we all needed to have a family reunion. And oh, the correspondence that went back and forth about a week in Breckenridge. We now lived in the technology age, where practically every home has a computer. E-mails ruled. Day in and day out, correspondence flowed and Rob sent pictures—wonderful pictures of a condo in Breckenridge, owned by wealthy people who rented it out for the summer months. "Let's do it!" was the final consensus. And we did.

Our son, now living in Houston with his family, did the driving in a Suburban that accommodated his family plus Bud and me, and we traveled the long miles with excitement and joy. What a glorious way for older parents to spend a week with their three children and six grandchildren. Just sitting in the back seat of the car coloring with Ryne and Gracie, Dave and Margaret's two children, was the highlight of my day. Gracie was three at the time and Ryne five.

When we arrived at the condo, we felt overwhelmed with the beauty we saw. How uncomfortable can you be in a living arrangement that has two fireplaces, seven bedrooms, five baths, and five refrigerators? The huge kitchen had two dishwashers and a granite counter that wrapped around cabinets and could accommodate at least eight people.

We attended the Fourth of July Parade that crowded the streets of Breckenridge, and enjoyed hot dogs, pop, and numerous delectable treats. But we didn't know that trouble awaited us when we returned home. I knew that Jack was going through a bad time. His breathing sounded labored and doctors once again considered heart surgery. When we left for Breckenridge, I knew that consultations were going on, but no decision had been made.

Just a few days earlier, I asked Marie to take the phone number for Breckenridge in case of an emergency.

"That's not necessary, Helen," she said. "He'll be all right. Call me when you get back."

She had such faith in his doctors that it never occurred to her that anything could happen.

I insisted she take the phone number. When the ring startled us, I knew. Somehow, I knew why it was ringing. It was their son, John, telling us that his dad, Jack George Kedzie, born December 15, 1925, had passed into eternity on July 4, 2001. He went into surgery, but never made it through.

To say we sobbed, is putting it mildly. We all gave way to throaty and guttural cries. We loved this man and never ever thought his time would run out. We drove back to Chicago with Karen to attend the funeral.

We little knew that morning,
God was going to call your name.
In life we loved you dearly,
In death we do the same.

After fifty years of marriage, Jack was gone and Marie was alone. She found comfort in that big house and decided to stay there. A decent and reliable new tenant had recently moved in upstairs, and that satisfied her as she found enjoyment and laughter in her loving sons, daughters-in-law, and grandchildren. But a murmur came from a source unknown that said, "I want you with me."

Marie and Jack Kedzie's family

She didn't hear the murmur at first. She moved along comfortably taking care of financial problems, paying doctors and hospital bills, running her home, and even, after a few months buying a new car. She and I talked on the phone once a week. Her laughter returned. She was doing fine.

"I'm going to Brooke's birthday party," she told me one day. "My darling little granddaughter will be five years old." She moved confidently and peacefully through her life, and we all remarked how well she was doing.

A phone call one morning brought a different story.

"I've got to have some blood work done. I'm not feeling too well," she confided as I sipped coffee sitting on the bar stool in the kitchen. "I've talked to Dr. Clark and he wants a complete blood report."

"Call me and let me know the results, okay?" I said.

I didn't hear from her, but she stayed on my mind a whole

week. Finally, I called her.

"Well, what's the verdict? Did you have the blood work done?" I asked. Her hesitation scared me.

"My blood count is very low," she answered. "The range for platelets is not what it should be. I have to have the test done again to reinforce their diagnosis."

"What's their diagnosis?" I asked.

"They think it's leukemia."

My eyes closed and I froze up inside.

"That's not even in our family," I said. "How in heaven's name could you have that?"

"I don't know," she answered.

But the second testing confirmed that Marie had leukemia. I talked to friends who said, "Oh, my father has had that for twenty years. He lives each day just fine."

I talked to another woman in my writing group that had it, and even took the chemo. She survived beautifully.

I felt encouraged and passed all this information on to her each time we talked.

"You're going to be all right," I said as my heart thumped and my throat tightened. "I'm praying for you and the Lord has never let me down."

She turned to a female leukemia specialist at Rush-Presbyterian Hospital. Dr. Lackery was determined to save Marie and tried every type of medical experiment possible, but nothing deterred the inevitable. Marie lost most of her hair and my heart broke over this. Since childhood, she had always had the most beautiful curly hair.

"I've bought a wig," she told me on one of my many phone calls to her early in the morning.

"How's it look?" I asked.

She wasn't totally sold on it. Most times she either ran around the house bald or wore a kerchief. When someone rang the doorbell, she'd wrap her head in a towel and pretend she'd just left the shower. I tried to encourage floral headdresses in loud colors. Pictures sent through e-mail showed her looking great in the wig, but she didn't think so. "Besides," she said, "It's just too darn hot."

Sometimes she seemed cheerful, sometimes confused, oftentimes curious about how all of this would turn out. Never was she sad, morbid, or complaining. I continued my constant phone calls.

"I feel fine," she said. "How can I be so sick?"

"Marie, I'm coming to Chicago, " I said. "I want to spend some time with you and when you come home from the hospital, I'll be there to help you."

Her hospital stay lasted a couple of weeks and they finally released her after relieving the leg swelling and body rash she suffered. Chemo was discontinued.

Karen picked me up at O'Hare International Airport. I spent a few days with her and her family. Marie, still claiming she felt okay, had us over for lunch. She made eggplant Parmesan, one of our favorites, and we enjoyed a rich and fulfilling afternoon. When Karen left, I remained.

I helped her more than I thought I'd have to, discovering that she needed assistance putting on her socks and shoes; just dressing in the morning was a chore for her. I insisted on running down to the basement to do the laundry. I wanted to preserve her, keep her well. I vowed to do anything to make her well. A couple of times she braved driving to the grocery store and pushed the grocery cart with difficulty. I finally convinced her to pick up the items she wanted and I'd push the cart. Her body seemed to fail more each day, but because of her cheerful good nature on the phone, I was not aware of this.

Bud called often. "How is she today?" he'd ask.

"Not any better than yesterday," I'd answer.

One evening as she sat bundled up in a quilt—she was always cold—she asked me a question.

"Have you watched The Sopranos?"

"No," I answered. "We don't get HBO with our cable connection."

"The boys gave me the complete set of videos for Christmas. Would you like to see one?"

"Well, I understand there's a lot of sex and violence. I'm not so sure I want to watch it."

"You're old enough," she said. "Put this one in." She reached down next to her chair and handed me a video.

I put the video in and sat back to watch and listen to a four-letter word repeated constantly.

"Gosh, Marie, the swearing is unbelievable."

"Wait," she said. "It gets better as time goes on."

I had to smile at that.

By the end of the first video I was hooked. Every evening, after a great dinner, we sat comfortably in lounge chairs to watch *The Sopranos*. Halfway through, she fell asleep. When the video ended, I guided her to bed and prayed she'd have a good night sleep.

Chapter 37

"Michael, this is Aunt Helen."

"Yeah?" answered Michael.

"Your mother is running a temperature. It's over 101. What should we do?" I asked nervously.

"We'll have to take her to the hospital," he sighed dejectedly.

Marie's youngest son, Michael, had studied to be a doctor at one time before he became a lawyer, so he knew the seriousness of her condition. At eleven o'clock that night, we bundled up Marie and drove to Rush-Presbyterian Hospital.

Just months before, Bud and I had entered his ninety-four-year old mother into a nursing home in Texas because of a serious fall she took in her backyard. She didn't survive. We attended her funeral on August 22, 2002.

Now, here again, running back and forth to a hospital became my top priority as we watched nurses and doctors in the emergency ward rush and work in order to make Marie comfortable. She trembled with chills, yet her body temperature kept rising. Now it was close to 103 degrees and the hospital staff worked diligently to lower the fever.

Doctors and nurses came into the emergency room off and on, not telling us anything. They covered her while she shook with cold and uncovered her when she burned from heat. She lay stretched straight out, with pale long-veined fingers clutching a white sheet. Finally, a head nurse came in, bundled Marie in blankets, and told us to go home. They were moving her to a private room and would sedate her for the night, she said.

"No need for you to stay. She'll be all right and you can see her in the morning." Michael and I left exhausted, at four o'clock in the morning after they stabilized the temperature and put her in the private room.

Falling asleep instantly after returning to Marie's house would have been a blessing, but that didn't happen. I sat in that big house by myself, worried sick about her. The house noises startled me. Twice I reached down to the side of the bed for my slippers and walked to the front window to look out at the dark night. Early dawn found me looking out a back window, waiting anxiously for the morning to come. I prayed. Oh how I prayed.

But once again Marie bounced back and after two weeks, I returned home to Texas.

"Go on home," she told me. "I'll be fine. That was just a delayed reaction to the chemo."

The month of September in Texas continued to bring scorching temperatures. It was cool and pleasant in Chicago, so Bud and I decided once again to drive the fifteen hundred miles to Chicago to visit Karen, family, and close friends. The drives from Georgetown to Chicago seemed to take forever, but we enjoyed stopping at a motel the first night and then generally arriving at Karen's after lunch. All were excited about seeing Grandpa Bud, since he hadn't visited Chicago in a while, but my thoughts focused on seeing Marie.

Before we left, she had started a program of medications encouraged by Dr. Lackery, who told her to take six pills a day. Marie and I talked about the severity of this many times over the phone.

"Six pills a day. Are you sure?" I asked.

"Yes," she said. "I started thinking I should take one a day.

When I went in to have blood work done, I saw Dr. Lackery and her assistant. They remarked how great I looked.

I told them I feel fine and am taking that pill every day."

"Taking a pill, Marie?" the doctor asked. "You should be taking six a day." Oh my, how I worried about that.

When we reached Chicago, I wondered if the leukemia or the six pills were killing her. Her body locked up, her bowels stopped functioning, and clearly she was failing. We watched day in and day out as Marie lay in the hospital dying a slow death. Buddy, Karen, and I stood at her bedside with Michael, Mary, Karen, Philip, Florence, and all the other members of the family stroking her arm and holding her hand as we watched her make peace with her God.

When Bobby arrived from California, his heart broke to find his mother in such a state. Finally, after days of suffering, the family decided to remove the machines and let her go. She died around 9:30 pm September 29, 2002. It was a Sunday. John, Cathy, and Bobby sat with her at the end as she peacefully said goodbye.

To quote her son Bob: "We were talking to her about having a bowl of ice cream, which she loved while watching TV late at night. And the last forty minutes or so she seemed not to be fighting to breathe. Everything was so calm and she simply slipped off to be with the love of her life, Dad."

To this day, I find it hard to believe she's gone. A day or night doesn't go by that I don't think about her. But one consolation, extremely important to us, is that she was surrounded by so much love in her final days.

Bobby contends that the murmur I mentioned earlier came from his Dad, Jack. "He wanted her with him, Aunt Helen."

I believe it.

We stood together at the Visitation. All of the family assembled in a large room filled with the aroma of roses and various floral arrangements. Chairs were provided and people came and went. But after a while people just kept coming in until the room filled up and overflowed into another room. She was loved and respected by many. Neighbors, friends, and relatives all turned out as she lay in a white satin coffin, sleeping peacefully in a red jacket. A rosary encircled her folded hands. Her brown curly hair had returned as lovely as ever.

Then we all turned as our brother Joe, at eighty-three, came through the crowd with his son, Tom. He was not a well man himself as he leaned on a cane, but his brilliant smile took our minds off of his illness as we gathered him in our arms to welcome him. It had been a long journey for them to make, Tom coming from California to bring his Dad from way southwest Lisle to Irving Park Road, Chicago's north side. Joe's Mary, crippled with arthritis, couldn't share this moment with us. But we certainly felt her there with us in spirit.

Seeing Joe, we laughed and cried and remembered. This handsome man, now suffering from Crohn's disease, seemed so fresh and vibrant, even though pale in color. I didn't want to leave his side, and kept recalling memories of a marriage where two young people met secretly just to be together. And now after more than sixty years, it was the first time I'd seen them apart.

I came to treasure this time with him, for more than two months later on Saturday, November 11th in the same year, 2002, we sadly assembled again at a memorial visitation for Joe at Blake-Lamb Funeral Home in Lisle, Illinois. A military funeral complete with "Taps" carried him on his way to eternity as two Marines gave him their final salute. Six months after Joe's death, Mary at eighty-four relocated to California to live near her son and daughter-in-law.

> Loving and kind in all his ways.
> Upright and just to the end of days;
> Sincere and true in his heart and mind,
> A beautiful memory he left behind.

But again a murmur occurred, this time from Joe to Mary. After Mary had lived five months in California near her family, an e-mail arrived telling us that Mary passed away on a Wednesday morning at Manor Care nursing facility in Encinitas. Her son Tom reported seeing her the Sunday before, when he found her doing fine and asking to get out of bed because she wanted to be more active. But it was just a last spurt of energy, for in just a matter of days she died peacefully in her sleep.

Mary also was cremated, and her ashes reside next to Joe's at Fort Rosecranes near the Marine Core Reserve Depot in California.

Joe and Mary

Chapter 38

When I finally found time to think and reflect, I had to accept that my parents and siblings were gone. At age seventy-three, I was the only one left. Florence sold her home and moved into a condo not far from River Forest. I could call or visit her from time to time, but Marie was a great loss. She blended laughter and tears so skillfully no one else could match her. She could love you today and hate you tomorrow, but that was her way. She never brought permanent sorrow.

More and more, I find myself reflecting on my growing-up days in Chicago in the forties. Visiting many years later, I found many changes. Some of the well-kept homes had been torn down, and empty lots full of weeds and broken beer bottles took their places. Gone were the lively hearts that emerged each morning to welcome the sunshine or snow, depending on the time of year. The Victory Garden on the corner that the whole block helped to plant during World War II, sat barren and dead, with only prickly dandelion leaves surviving. I felt saddened by the sprawling deterioration and mourned for the vibrant neighborhood I grew up in.

Passing Mrs. Martin's two-story brick house, my heart sank as I pictured her kneeling to plant the bright impatiens and petunias that flourished every June. Fresh curtains hung on her clothesline routinely every spring as she cleaned and freshened her windows. Now the house badly needed repairs and paint. I saw no curtains on the windows, only a crack that ran across the bottom of a pane.

I brightened, though, when I saw the green fence that still ran the length of Flournoy Street. It was faded now with loose boards, but still standing, reminding me of the times I ran sticks along it many years ago just to enjoy the noise. If I recall rightly, there used to be a fire truck behind the green fence, and the fire department made a special effort to paint the fence every couple of years. The fence's dilapidated condition revealed that no one took that special care now.

Standing on the corner of Flournoy and Claremont on this particular day, I smiled and grew excited when I looked down the block to see that our old house still stood there. I began strolling toward it and then ran, wanting to get there faster.

I saw from afar the several stairs leading up to the front porch, and recognized the wrought-iron railings on each side. Seeing them reminded me of the bench on the porch where Mom sat on cool summer evenings after dishes, just to see what was going on. Ladies stood gossiping and boys played tag while girls hop-scotched down chalk squares.

Standing at the bottom looking up the stairs, I noticed the pretty front door with its side glass windows, still sturdy. Mom always had sheer gathered curtains on the windows, but today they were bare. However, the house still remained elegant looking despite the faded yellow paint and wide crack that ran down the front brick stairs. The wrought-iron railing on one side was missing. From where I stood, the house looked unoccupied.

I tiptoed up the stairs and peeked in the side glass panel on the left of the door. There I glimpsed a wonderful panorama of memories, a parade of days and moments that told a story. Images appeared. I saw Mom at the foot of the long flight of stairs calling up to come down for dinner, Marie in the kitchen setting the table, Daddy reading his newspaper.

As I turned to leave that day, the sunlight caught my eye and transported me back to my childhood.

The family in Breckenridge, Colorado

Appendix

The Dunn Family Tree

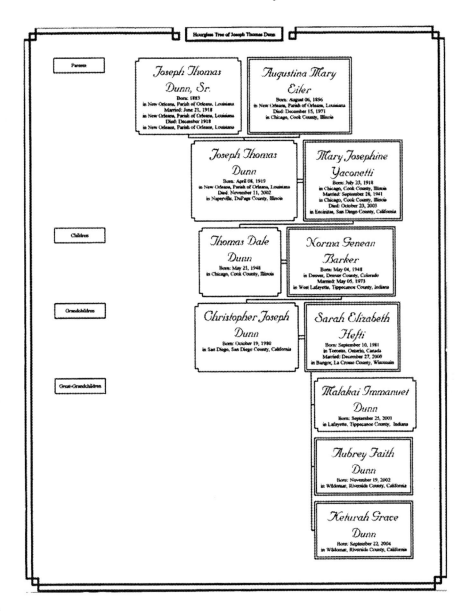

Hourglass Tree of Joseph Thomas Dunn

Parents

Joseph Thomas Dunn, Sr.
Born: 1883
in New Orleans, Parish of Orleans, Louisiana
Married: June 21, 1918
in New Orleans, Parish of Orleans, Louisiana
Died: December 1918
in New Orleans, Parish of Orleans, Louisiana

Augustina Mary Eiler
Born: August 06, 1896
in New Orleans, Parish of Orleans, Louisiana
Died: December 15, 1971
in Chicago, Cook County, Illinois

Joseph Thomas Dunn
Born: April 08, 1919
in New Orleans, Parish of Orleans, Louisiana
Died: November 11, 2002
in Naperville, DuPage County, Illinois

Mary Josephine Yaconetti
Born: July 23, 1918
in Chicago, Cook County, Illinois
Married: September 28, 1941
in Chicago, Cook County, Illinois
Died: October 23, 2003
in Encinitas, San Diego County, California

Children

Thomas Dale Dunn
Born: May 21, 1948
in Chicago, Cook County, Illinois

Norma Genean Barker
Born: May 04, 1948
in Denver, Denver County, Colorado
Married: May 05, 1973
in West Lafayette, Tippecanoe County, Indiana

Grandchildren

Christopher Joseph Dunn
Born: October 19, 1980
in San Diego, San Diego County, California

Sarah Elizabeth Hefti
Born: September 10, 1981
in Toronto, Ontario, Canada
Married: December 27, 2000
in Bangor, La Crosse County, Wisconsin

Great-Grandchildren

Malakai Immanuel Dunn
Born: September 25, 2001
in Lafayette, Tippecanoe County, Indiana

Aubrey Faith Dunn
Born: November 19, 2002
in Wildomar, Riverside County, California

Keturah Grace Dunn
Born: September 22, 2004
in Wildomar, Riverside County, California

221

The Zimardo Family

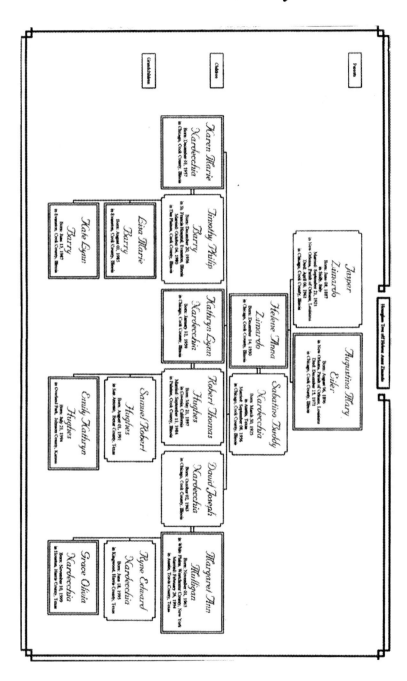

To order additional copies of
Remembering the Early Years
or
Sophie and Ben
by Helen Nardecchia

Name _____

Address _____

_____

_____

Remembering the Early Years
$16.95 x _____ copies =   _____

Sophie and Ben
$12.95 x _____ copies =   _____

Sales Tax   _____
(Texas residents add 8.25% sales tax)

Please add $3.50 postage and handling
and an additional $1 for each additional book   _____

Total amount due: _____

Please send check or money order for books to:

WordWright.biz, Inc.
P.O. Box 9770
Alpine, TX 79831

For a complete catalog of books,
visit our site at
http://www.WordWright.biz